Emerging from the infinite gloom was a portion of a haunting figure, a grotesque display of pain and hatred. This countenance, gnarled by time and torment, was all too familiar to Nancy. It was Jimmy Smazmoth, now known to most by the cruel epithet, "Smash-Mouth," a name earned not in jest or camaraderie but borne out of violence from teammates who, in a frenzied moment, had brutally assaulted him, shattering his jaw. That mutilated mandible hung precariously, a pendulous reminder of not only the brutalities he had endured but the brutalities committed in his honor.

In this vision, however, Jimmy was not the victim. His eyes locked onto Nancy with an intensity that froze her to the spot. From his maw, a viscous yellow saliva dripped in rhythm with his steps. The old athletic tape that once bound his cracking hands now seemed fused to his flesh. The sight was undoubtedly as unpleasant as anything she had witnessed, but it was almost exclusively the latent intent behind those unblinking eyes that petrified Nancy.

END ZONE 2

Written by Jean Chiles Tempi

Based on a Screenplay by L. Ray Hobbson

Based on a story by Warren Q. Harolds

END ZONE 2 is an original publication of Launch Over Books. This work has never appeared before in book form. This work is a novel. Any similarity to actual persons or events is entirely coincidental.

LAUNCH OVER BOOKS
A division of Launch Over LLC
Hollywood, CA 90068

First Launch Over Printing, August 2024

Printed in the U. S. A.

FOREWORD

In the summer of 2017 in Sheboygan, Wisconsin, a collector of rare James Dean films stumbled upon a dusty box containing the first reel of an Italian print of the lost cult horror film *End Zone 2* mislabeled as the classic Sally Field TV series, *The Flying Nun*. Beneath the reel, wrapped in crumbling, yellowing parchment, lay the scattered manuscript of the novelization of *End Zone 2*.

This discarded adaptation was penned by Jean Chiles Tempi during a single, feverish weekend in 1969, months before the film's completion. Commissioned by her lover, producer Jacques Renault, just weeks before his mysterious death, the manuscript was shelved indefinitely when coroner Tex Beckerson, who acquired the rights, told Jean, "No one likes to read," and canceled the publication.

Jean remained determined to convince Tex that the book would be a hit, adding a scattershot final chapter to meet his demands of "more cannibalism and more football," but Tex was unswayed, and the book was still not to be...until now!

From the depths of obscurity, we present the novelization, just as Ms. Tempi had hoped it would appear in 1970. Prepare for a descent into the macabre, where past sins and haunting memories collide in a battle for survival.

END ZONE 2

PROLOGUE

George Donner was born on March 7, 1784, in North Carolina into a family of German descent. His parents, George Donner Sr. and Mary Huff Donner, were pioneers in their own right, embodying a spirit of adventure and resilience that would later characterize George's own life. Growing up in that family of frontiersmen, George was imbued with a sense of exploration and a drive to carve out a life in the burgeoning American frontier.

George was known for his industrious nature and his knack for leadership, qualities that earned him respect in his community. His early years were marked by an untiring pursuit of prosperity, a trait that would eventually lead him to undertake one of the most ill-fated journeys in American history and, more than 100 years later, inspire others to commit acts of inconceivable violence.

By the mid-1830s, Donner and his wife, whose name remains unknown to this day, had relocated to Illinois along with their children. George continued to farm there, but the westward expansion of the United States, spurred by the promise of fertile land and new opportunities, captured George's imagination. In particular, the lure of California, with its affluent agricultural prospects, was irresistible. In addition, the declaration of America's "Manifest Destiny" to conquer the remaining frontier implied that anyone who chose to undertake the dangerous task was serving not only themselves but their country. At age 60, when most men of his time would have settled into a quieter life if they were still living, George Donner led his family on a perilous journey.

In the spring of 1846, George Donner, his third wife Tamsen Donner, and his brother Jacob took their families to join a larger group of emigrants bound for California. The party, later known as the Donner Party after Donner had become the troupe's leader, set out with high hopes and dreams of a better life. Little did they know, their journey would soon become one of the most tragic tales of the American frontier and a symbol of the high price of freedom and prosperity.

Like many other westward migrations, the Donner Party's journey began with optimism and determination. They traveled through Illinois, Iowa, and Nebraska, following well-trodden paths along the Platte River. However, the decision to take a newly established route, the Hastings Cutoff, was their fatal error.

In 1846, Lansford Warren Hastings wrote *The Emigrants' Guide to Oregon and California,* a book intended to provide essential information and encouragement to prospective settlers embarking on the arduous journey westward to Oregon and California. In this guide, Hastings emphasized the natural beauty and potential ease of travel of the cutoff he named for himself.

In a classic case of "do not believe everything you read," the Hastings Cutoff first took the Donner Party through the arid Great Salt Lake Desert, where they suffered from a lack of water and food. The grueling conditions and extended journey sapped their strength and depleted their resources. By the time they reached the Sierra Nevada mountains in late October, winter had set in with a vengeance.

A severe and seasonally early snowstorm trapped the Donner Party in the Sierra Nevada near what is now

Truckee, California. Unable to advance or retreat, they were forced to make camp and wait for a break in the weather. The group split into several smaller camps around Truckee Lake—renamed Donner Lake some forty years ago—and Alder Creek, where they hastily constructed makeshift shelters from the cold.

As the weeks turned into months, the snow did not relent, and the situation grew dire. Food supplies dwindled, and the pioneers faced starvation. With no options left, they consumed their remaining livestock, hides, bones, and even bark. However, these meager rations were not enough. As members of the party began to die from malnutrition and exposure, the survivors faced an unimaginable choice—resort to cannibalism or perish.

The decision to consume the flesh of the dead was not taken lightly. It was borne out of sheer desperation and the instinct to survive. George Donner, who by this time was incapacitated by an infected wound, was among those who faced this horrifying reality.

The travelers were all too familiar with the Biblical framing of the consumption of the dead. Leviticus chapter 26 said a cannibalistic curse would be placed on those who walked contrary to the Lord. "You shall eat the flesh of your sons, and you shall eat the flesh of your daughters," this passage read. The Donners feared their journey and their prioritization of Nation over devoutness had gone against God and that in response to this lapse in faith and judgment, they were disciplined sevenfold for their sins, as Leviticus warned.

With faith shaken, George's leadership and resolve, which had guided the group thus far, could no longer shield them from the brutality of nature and the consequences of their ill-fated choices. Small groups attempted to find help, including the Forlorn Hope, a group of fifteen who set out on snowshoes to seek rescue. Only seven of them survived, but their journey alerted others to the plight of the stranded emigrants.

In February 1847, the first of several rescue parties arrived. Over the next few months, rescuers braved the treacherous conditions to bring the survivors to safety. By the time the last rescue party arrived in April, only 48 of the original 87 members of the Donner Party were still alive.

George Donner, however, was not among them. He died in March 1847 at Alder Creek, unable to be moved due to a gangrenous injury to his hand. His wife, Tamsen Donner, stayed by his side until the end despite opportunities to leave with earlier rescue parties. Tamsen ultimately perished as well, leaving their children orphaned but among the survivors.

William Fallon, the leader of the group dispatched to salvage the remains of the Donner Party, described an appallingly grim scene. According to Fallon, Lewis Keseberg claimed to be the sole survivor remaining at the small camp where George and Tamsen Donner had died. Fallon also recounted that Keseberg explained how Tamsen Donner had become disoriented on her journey from the Alder Creek camp to the lake cabins. She spent excessive time outside in the snow, barely making it to Keseberg's cabin before succumbing to the elements shortly after. Fallon's account goes deliciously further, alleging that Keseberg resorted to cannibalizing Donner and even declared that her flesh was "the best he had ever tasted."

For better or worse, the Donner Party became a symbol of the extremes of human endurance and the dark side of the American pioneer spirit. George Donner's name, forever linked to this tragic tale, evokes both the determination that drives individuals to seek new horizons and the perilous consequences of hubris and miscalculation.

Donner's legacy is complex. On one hand, he represents the quintessential pioneer, driven by dreams of prosperity and a better life. On the other, his decisions—particularly the choice to take the Hastings Cutoff—underscore the perilous risks inherent in the westward expansion, abandonment of sanctity, and the realization of America's "Manifest Destiny."

History looks upon those who carried out the Nation's expansive will as heroes and martyrs, rarely considering the price the Native men, women, and children paid.

In the early 1950s, two independent phenomena set the stage for the memory of the Donners to return to public consciousness. First, an inexplicable fascination with cannibalism began to percolate through certain quarters of the American psyche. Post-war America, amidst its suburban boom and burgeoning consumer culture, found itself confronted by the darker recesses of its past, perhaps as a means of confronting the more primal aspects of human nature that had been unleashed during the global conflict.

Second, after centuries of removal, relocation, and elimination, the early 1950s marked the peak of the Indian termination movement, a virtual mandate of abandonment of tribal communities in favor of receiving the rights and, more importantly, the obligations of all American citizens. Government-orchestrated propaganda programs associated with this cause encouraged communities in the Western United States to look back into their history and unearth opportunities to celebrate pioneers and frontiersmen.

During this period of frontier history revival, Walt Disney produced the Davey Crockett television series and built the Frontierland section of the new Disneyland theme park. Whether Frontierland was a part of Disney's original plans for the park or whether it was constructed under a mandate from the government in exchange for granting the right to build the park is a matter seemingly lost to history.

In these multifaceted contexts, the bloody tale of the Donner Party resurfaced in the public consciousness, captivating the morbid curiosity of a new generation. This strange fascination found an outlet in a quiet, unassuming town in California nestled in the Sierra Nevada mountains. In this seemingly placid locale, a group of local citizens, driven by a bizarre mix of dark humor, historical interest, nationalism stirred by the fear of communism, and a plain old desire to attract attention, proposed naming the new high school after George Donner.

The ombudsmen meeting where the decision was made was anything but ordinary. Most similar sessions were barely attended by those with a mandate. This meeting drew an unusually large crowd comprising nearly every local citizen in the old town hall. The proposal to name the high school after George Donner was initially met with incredulous laughter. Yet, as the discussion progressed and arguments were presented, the mood shifted. Proponents of the idea argued that naming the school after Donner would serve as a unique historical reminder, a way to ensure that the tragic lessons of the past were not forgotten. They painted a picture of resilience and determination, highlighting the endurance of the human spirit even in the face of unimaginable hardship.

Opponents, on the other hand, were appalled by the suggestion, deeming it in poor taste. They pointed out the grim reality of the cannibalism that had occurred and argued that it was an inappropriate legacy for a place of learning. However, as the debate wore on, it became clear that the proponents had tapped into a peculiar vein of fascination and dark curiosity that resonated with the audience. The story of the Donner Party, with its gruesome details and harrowing survival narrative, had an undeniable allure. Those against it were also unfairly deemed communist sympathizers by the "for" camp.

The meeting culminated in a heated vote. The result was close, but ultimately, the proponents prevailed. The high school would be named George Donner High School. The decision sent ripples through the community, sparking both outrage and amusement. It was not long before news of the unusual naming decision spread beyond their sleepy community, drawing the attention of newspapers and radio stations. The town found itself in the spotlight, with journalists and curious onlookers flocking to the area. Sadly, as you will soon discover, this would not be the last time the town received such attention.

The high school's official dedication ceremony was a spectacle in itself. Held on a crisp autumn day, it featured speeches from local dignitaries who extolled those same virtues of resilience and the importance of remembering history presented at the voting meeting. A large plaque bearing George Donner's name and a brief account of the Donner Party's tragic journey was unveiled. Students and teachers alike were left to ponder the strange and somber legacy that their school now carried.

The school's sports team, the Donner Pioneers, played under the shadow of their namesake's grim tale. The library amassed a unique collection of books and artifacts related to the Donner Party, drawing researchers and history enthusiasts from far and wide.

While certainly never the intention, there is little doubt that the moniker nurtured a fascination with cannibalism and flesh consumption among its constituency. The shadow of the Donner Party loomed large over George Donner High School, casting an eerie pall over the town and its inhabitants. The peculiar choice of name created an atmosphere where the devilish history of cannibalism and survival against all odds became an intrinsic part of the school's identity and seeped into the collective psyche of its students.

Jimmy Smazmoth was one such student, profoundly influenced by the legacy of his school. Growing up in a town that took peculiar pride in a dark history, he found himself both repelled and fascinated by the stories of the Donner Party. Jimmy was a bright student, but he often felt like an outsider. The school's history became an outlet for his burgeoning sense of teenage alienation and anger.

The football team, revered as local heroes, embodied the high school's spirit. Their successes on the field were celebrated with fervor, and their players were held in high regard. But beneath the surface, the football team harbored a culture of bullying and elitism. Jimmy, who already felt marginalized, became a frequent target of their torment. The players taunted him with the very history that the town and school so perversely celebrated, making crude jokes about cannibalism and flesh-eating at his expense.

As this bullying intensified, Jimmy's fascination with the Donner Party's history took a darker turn. He began to draw parallels between himself and the ill-fated pioneers, seeing himself as a victim of circumstance, pushed to the edge by those in power. His isolation deepened, and he spent hours in the school library, poring over books about the Donner Party in the special collection, particularly drawn to the stories of survival and revenge. The line between historical interest and obsession blurred, and Jimmy's thoughts became increasingly consumed by notions of retribution.

The constant bullying and his growing obsession with the Donner Party eventually reached a tipping point. Jimmy's mental state deteriorated, his thoughts debauched by the relentless provocation and the dark allure of vengeance. He began to see the football team not just as his tormentors but as symbols of a broader injustice that demanded retribution. In his mind, they were the modern-day equivalents of those who had driven the Donner Party to their desperate fate.

Jimmy's mother, Angela Smazmoth, was close with the boy and acutely aware of her son's suffering. She had watched helplessly as the light in his eyes dimmed, replaced by a haunted look of despondency and anger. Angela, too, was no stranger to the town's dark history and the unaccountable pride it took in its morbid legacy. She had always harbored a fierce protective instinct for her son, and seeing him pushed to the brink awakened a primal fury within her.

When the team severely beat Jimmy in response to a rumor that he was more well endowed than the quarterback, Angela could no longer stand idly by. As a result of his dislocated jaw, which doctors said would never heal, Jimmy could no longer eat solid food. Jimmy quickly grew thin and frail and lacked the nutrients he needed to remain alive.

As Jimmy's condition worsened, Angela's thoughts turned increasingly toward vengeance. The idea of those who had hurt her son living without consequence became unbearable. The stories of the Donner Party, particularly the tales of survival at any cost, resonated deeply with her. She saw herself as a modern-day avenger, much like the desperate pioneers who had resorted to extreme measures to survive.

The championship game, a night meant for celebration and school spirit, became the setting for Angela's heinous vendetta. Determined to hide her identity, she dressed up as a malformed and terrifying figure based on the nickname "Smash-Mouth," which was given to Jimmy after the beating, as well as his actual disfigured appearance. She believed channeling a demonic variant of Jimmy would strike fear into her victims and give her the strength and courage to get revenge.

Wearing a mask and costume, Angela ambushed the football team in the locker room. The attack was swift and brutal, fueled by years of pent-up rage and a distorted sense of righteousness. Angela's actions were not just an act of personal revenge but a symbolic strike against the culture that had celebrated the very legacy of cannibalism that had become her obsession.

The massacre sent shockwaves through the town. The high school, which had once reveled in its dark history, now faced the horrifying reality of history's consequences. Angela's actions were condemned, and the town grappled with the implications. The celebration of the Donner Party had influenced one of their own.

In the aftermath, it was Nancy, a cheerleader and one of the football team's supporters, who ultimately confronted Angela. Driven by fear, anger, and a desperate need to end the nightmare, Nancy tracked Angela down. The confrontation was intense and brutal. Still dressed as "Smash-Mouth," Angela fought with the ferocity of someone with nothing to lose. But Nancy, fueled by a determination to protect her friends and stop the madness, managed to overpower her.

In the final moments of their struggle, Nancy was forced to kill Angela by stabbing her 25 times to save herself and end the reign of terror. Angela's death marked the end of a horrifying chapter for the town, but the scars left behind by her actions and the twisted legacy of George Donner High School would linger for years to come.

Now, on the 15th anniversary of the death of Angela Smazmoth and the 123rd anniversary of the death of Tamsen Eustis Dozier Donner, our story begins.

CHAPTER 1: A TALE OF TWO REALITIES

It was the worst of times. It was the worst of times. It was the age of foolishness. It was the age of ignorance. It was the epoch of disbelief. It was the epoch of terror. It was the season of darkness. It was the season of desolation. It was the winter of despair. It was the winter of utter hopelessness. In the dimly lit room, the radio announcer's voice promising tranquil weather ahead for the earliest winter days fought to overcome the static. Nancy filled her suitcase, methodically picking out clothing from her démodé wardrobe, each piece an unintentional tribute to the styles of yesteryears. Outings requiring such thought were a rarity for her, especially one that would see her traveling hundreds of miles to meet up with her former Donner High cheerleading squad mates.

Fifteen years. That's how long it had been since the events that shadowed what should have been the bright conclusion of her senior year. The curtains were prematurely drawn on their academic lives that year; there were no final exams, no graduation gowns. For amidst the joy and anticipation, a dark tragedy had struck, leaving many lives shattered and dreams unfulfilled.

"Nancy, you were one of the fortunate ones," was the refrain she heard repeatedly, a comfort she had never felt. A decade and a half might have dulled the edges of her memories, but the scars? They remained raw and exposed. It felt like both forever and hardly an instant had passed.

Facing her former teammates, the girls with whom she once shared unbridled laughter and joy, felt daunting. And then there was Shelly. Time had frozen the moment when Angela Smazmoth's attack was cut short by Nancy, but not before Shelly's innocent sister, Brenda, met an unthinkable end; chopped up, blended, and fed to Angela's son, Jimmy. This made Shelly's invitation even more perplexing. Nancy and Shelly had not spoken at all in the intervening 15 years, and Nancy was sure that Shelly would still hold her responsible for Brenda's death. Was it an olive branch, or was it a trap? Either way, Nancy was sapped and ready to face the music.

As the radio announcer transitioned to a somber reflection of the tragedy, Nancy felt pulled back into a nothingness. Fifteen years to the day since the massacre at Donner High, the day that Nancy had become the reluctant heroine of that grim tale. The announcer recalled the story, intoning as if it were merely a myth. But to Nancy, it was all too real.

She felt like she was drowning, the burden of memories pulling her under. She not only had regular nightmares about that unescapable day but often slipped into horrifying daymares and hallucinations. When the announcer noted Nancy's name, specifying that she was responsible for killing Angela Smazmoth and putting an end to the massacre, Nancy sunk into her darkest and most lucid vision of horror ever.

She was back on the football field of Donner High, a place once permeated with cheers but now, in her vision, swallowed by fog. Under the ghostly glow of a full moon, Nancy, forever young in her dreams, executed her routines with a precision only marred slightly by the growing sense of dread. The jubilance of the cheers morphed slowly, the curve of her lips twisting from joy to something dark and repugnant. The sinister calls of her name, distant at first, grew more insistent, punctuated by an approaching rhythm of footsteps. She chanted louder, but even with screams and shouts, she could not drown out the hushed calls.

In the world of cheerleading, an unwritten code prevailed. Never let the facade crack. Never let the spirit waver. Yet on this particular night, Nancy, the ever-resilient spirit, finally faltered on the field for the very first time. From the murky depths of her consciousness, those quiet voices began to swell, taking on an unsettling resonance that felt almost palpable. The voices grew raspier, filled with immeasurable sinister intent. The sound crystallized into a silhouette, clad in shadows yet unmistakable in its menace.

Emerging from the infinite gloom was a portion of a haunting figure, a grotesque display of pain and hatred. This countenance, gnarled by time and torment, was all too familiar to Nancy. It was Jimmy Smazmoth, now known to most by the cruel epithet, "Smash-Mouth," a name earned not in jest or camaraderie but borne out of violence from teammates who, in a frenzied moment, had brutally assaulted him, shattering his jaw. That mutilated mandible hung precariously, a pendulous reminder of not only the brutalities he had endured but the brutalities committed in his honor.

In this vision, however, Jimmy was not the victim. His eyes locked onto Nancy with an intensity that froze her to the spot. From his maw, a viscous yellow saliva dripped in rhythm with his steps. The old athletic tape that once bound his cracking hands now seemed fused to his flesh. The sight was undoubtedly as unpleasant as anything she had witnessed, but it was almost exclusively the latent intent behind those unblinking eyes that petrified Nancy. This wasn't just a mindless predator on the hunt; a personal vendetta was at play. Revenge gleamed in his eyes, each stride toward his prey filled with purpose. Nancy was the embodiment of a debt that had to be settled.

Smash-Mouth grew closer and closer, soulless and unrelenting. As he desperately reached out to grab his mother's killer, his eyes showed just a tiny glimmer of pain and regret. Nancy caught a fragment of this fleeting expression as Smash-Mouth's filthy fingers grazed her hair on the journey toward her cheek. Just as his rough digits connected with her soft skin, reality interjected.

The hypnotic grip of her haunting memory was suddenly severed by a sharp burst of static from the radio. Gasping, Nancy fumbled with the dials. Her fingers trembled as she sought the familiar comfort of another station, hoping to drown out the permanent hold of her traumatic reverie. A melodious tune filled the room, redolent of hope and the promises of a bygone American dream. As those melodies of an optimistic age began to play, emotion welled up inside Nancy. The unshakable guilt would not permit her to succumb to nostalgic rumination. The reunion loomed, a confrontation with a past that refused to stay buried. But she was resolute. Though memories might cling like shadows, she would not let them shape the path ahead.

CHAPTER 2: CRIME AND RETRIBUTION

On an exceptionally cold evening late in December a young woman came out of the apartment in which she lodged in a city with no name, or at least a name that mattered to no one, and drove slowly, as though in hesitation, toward the mountains. In fact, Nancy had left the city hours ago but had yet to reconcile her mind and body in this venture. The rhythmic hum of the car engine, punctuated by the gravel crunching beneath the tires, was the only companion accompanying Nancy on her long journey. As the landscape changed, civilization seemed to recede, replaced by the untouched, sprawling vistas of nature. The road seemed to stretch endlessly before her. As the sun dipped low on the horizon, painting the sky in a palette of oranges and purples, she caught sight of it—a lone structure atop a hill, bathed in the soft glow of the fading day.

It was referred to as a "cabin" by Shelly's family, a humble name for a residence that sat majestically amidst acres of verdant expanse. While the edifice proudly proclaimed its presence against the backdrop of trees and meadows, it was the only trace of human habitation as far as the eye could see. The surroundings bore testimony to nature's grandeur, with the dense woods boasting trails that meandered, inviting exploration, and a tranquil lake that shimmered in the twilight. It was as if the cabin stood guard at the gateway between civilization and the untamed wilderness.

Unbeknownst to Nancy, as the evening's shroud descended, a hive of activity unfolded within the cabin, its inhabitants preparing fervently for her impending arrival.

The interior of the house told of an intriguing aesthetic. It bore the bounty of time and careful hands that had curated a collection that spoke of nature, both in its vitality and mortality. Furs draped over furniture and intricately carved wood pieces added warmth to the space. Yet, what was indeed striking was the juxtaposition of the serene ambiance with the more gaudy details. Few who entered gathered that it was the ultimate contradiction—a quaint, calming nature retreat filled with symbols and artifacts of death and mutilation. The most commanding of this dichotomy was the living room chandelier, an intricate still life of bleached, sharpened bones with stark white forms that refracted the room's light, casting a mesmerizing, almost supernatural waltz of shadows upon the walls. The allure of its artistry masked a more perilous detail. The rusted chain from which the kaleidoscopic fixture hung appeared fragile, as though it might snap at any moment. And so, as the room was imbued with eager conversations and hushed expectations of Nancy's entrance, that chandelier of Damocles hung precariously, a silent sentinel symbolic of the beauty and danger that awaited the cabin's occupants.

The cabin's interior, infused with the soft golden glow of the evening, was animated with familiar voices that had once traveled through the halls and locker room of Donner High. Dominating the conversation was Shelly, her bullishness undiminished by time. Her energy engulfed Linda, who had always seemed to choose to walk in Shelly's shadow. Their dynamics, set in their formative years, persisted even now. With childhood dreams of Broadway lights and ovations once upon a time, Linda had found herself cast into a different play—a perpetual supporting role beside the more forceful Shelly.

Nearby, a shimmering window pane framed the vain and self-preoccupied Mary. The soft radiance caught the ripples in her hair as she adjusted and readjusted it. Though her vanity was old news, the window wasn't merely a mirror tonight but a portal through which she awaited Nancy's imminent arrival.

Deborah reacted tacitly to the hum of conversations, the atmosphere of anticipation, and the oscillating dynamics of old friends. In stark contrast to the fervor around her, she appeared tranquil, lost in the pages of *Sisterhood is Powerful*, seemingly oblivious to the chatter around her.

But Shelly, in her proper dramatic form, had a knack for bringing everyone back to the present conversation, regardless of whether the topic was natural or conjured. With a voice that bore a contrived urgency, she declared, "Nancy should be here any minute!"

Mary snapped back to reality from gazing at her translucent likeness in the window. "I can't believe you got her to actually come," she murmured, astonishment evident.

Linda mischievously added, "Shelly can get anyone to do pretty much anything."

But Shelly was never one to let comments, no matter how benign, go unanswered. With a tone that dripped irritation, she shot back, "Shut up, Linda!"

Deborah lifted her gaze from her feminist tome, eyes sharp and seeking. "Mary," she said dryly, "I don't think you have to worry about your hair. I really doubt Nancy cares."

Mary's defensive wall crumbled, if only for a moment. "I haven't seen her in 15 years. I don't want her to think anything has changed," she confessed, her vulnerability peeking through.

Unyielding, Shelly retorted with her classic caustic humor. "Maybe you shouldn't have aged 15 years then."

Mary's spirit, though briefly dampened, wasn't quickly squashed. "Just because you haven't gotten any new clothes since high school doesn't mean you look the same either," she returned, her laughter a tad too forced.

Deborah, with her characteristic positivity, offered a compliment. "I think you both look choice."

The unexpected praise left Mary momentarily disoriented. "Thanks," she uttered, the sarcasm reflexive.

But the undercurrents of their interactions were merely distractions. Deborah's unflinching smile and intense gaze broke in deference to the elephant in the room—Nancy. "Shelly, give it to me straight. How did you get Nancy to agree to come?"

Shelly hesitated briefly, her revelation hanging in the air. "I told her it was a chance to finally free herself of the guilt," she admitted.

Still eager to offer an opinion, Linda added, "Plus, Nancy feels bad that she got Brenda killed."

A frustrated Shelly snapped at Linda. "You always find a way to be talking when you should be keeping your mouth shut," she spat. Attempting to rationalize her actions, she continued. "Linda's right, I guess. I told her it was her chance to make it up to me for Brenda."

Mary arched an eyebrow. "Nothing like using your dead sister to get what you want," she observed with great skepticism.

Deborah interjected, trying to steer the conversation toward a more positive direction. "What do you think we should say to Nancy? Or maybe not say to Nancy?"

Shelly replied with a hint of mystery, "Don't worry so much about it. I've got a bunch of activities planned."

Mary, still dispensing sarcasm, retorted, "Great. Can't wait to do some tie-dying."

Deborah returned her gaze to her book, noting, "I'm glad I brought my book for when things get weird."

"Nothing's gonna be any weirder than your book," Shelly reflected back.

Linda, accidentally revealing too much about Shelly's intentions, inquired, "What about how we plan to scare Nancy?"

Shelly shot her a dirty look. Deborah, her concern evident, asked, "What?"

"Just trying to help her with a little shock therapy," Shelly justified.

Deborah's voice became firmer, "She needs love and solidarity from her sisters, not some kind of kooky lobotomy."

Shelly argued, "Nancy needs to stop hiding from all of us and from the past. She needs to realize that this affected all of us."

Mary, stirring the pot, interjected, "I don't know how you get over stabbing someone's mother 25 times."

"Yeah, 24 is probably the limit," Deborah joked.

Missing the joke completely but looking for clarification on something she thought she shouldn't bring up, Linda asked, "Wait, did they ever find Jimmy?"

Dismissive as always, Shelly replied, "Who? Smash-Mouth? He died in the fire."

Yet Linda's voice, tinged with an edge of doubt, added, "I heard they never found his body."

Shelly, growing more irritated by the second, retorted, "Yeah, he's been hiding for 15 years, just waiting to return."

Deborah raised her eyebrows and teased, "Nancy's been hiding for 15 years. Why not Jimmy?"

Jumping on the playful speculation, Mary added, "They've probably been hiding together. Maybe they've got a whole freaky secret family."

Nervous laughter rippled through the room as they indulged in these darkly humorous musings, each woman dealing with their own fears and anxieties uniquely. The pending reunion with Nancy and the shared history they all carried weighed heavily on their minds, making them grasp onto anything that could distract them from the looming uncertainties of the night ahead.

Would this reunion serve as a healing touch for Nancy, or would it resurface old wounds and bring forth horrors from the past? Only time would tell.

CHAPTER 3: FOR WHOM THE BLENDER WHIRRS

Smash-Mouth lay flat on the brown, rotten wood floor of the shack, his chin detached from his skull on one side, and outside, high overhead, the wind blew in the tops of the pine trees. This eerie and dimly lit shack adorned with the relics of forgotten times served as an unlikely gathering point. Cobwebs hung like gossamer drapes, and the air was rank with mildew and decay. Old newspapers, yellowed and brittle with age, littered the floor, intoning secrets of a bygone era with every crinkling step. The creaking of the old wooden floorboards under the paper added to the feeling of unease, as if the very structure of the shack was protesting the dark deeds being plotted within.

It was in this setting, with the past telling its wicked tales, that AJ worked meticulously on a crude implement, modifying an old football into an instrument of confrontation. His hands moved with a precision borne of necessity, weaving a deadly quilt of leather and barbed wire. Each barb was placed with care, each strip of leather tightened with a silent oath of vengeance.

AJ's face was penumbral, yet even through this nebulous form, his purpose in every deft movement was evident. His voice, though restrained, betrayed a passion that had been simmering for too long. "I saw them arrive, too. This is our chance to end this once and for all," he muttered, his words carrying the load of years of resentment and unresolved anger.

Amidst this oppressive gloom, a Hadean laugh echoed, chilling the air. It was a sound that seemed to come from the depths of the nullity, a cackle of pure malevolence. As if summoned by this call, a revolting living relic unveiled itself from the stygian corners—a lone jaw illuminated by the flickering candlelight, dripping in fetid ooze. This grim memento of a fate that had blurred the line between life and death was an attestation to the horrors that had birthed it.

Its laughter was a vile parody of joy—a reminder of the unnatural existence it now led. This horrifying apparition was Smash-Mouth, a being that defied the boundaries of reality and unreality, lurking in the shadows, ready to wreak havoc once more. His eyes glowed with a merciless light, a burning hatred that had festered for years, feeding off the memories of torment and pain.

Those who teased and mocked his limited intellectual and physical abilities could never, in their nightmares, have imagined that their cruel playground ballet could birth a being of such unspeakable horrors from the carapacial skin and football helmet of Jimmy Smazmoth. There were no longer any memories of Jimmy's childhood joys in this shape. All that was left was a vessel of rage fueled by vengeance for his beloved mother's violent demise.

AJ paused in his work, looking up at Smash-Mouth. "We've waited long enough, Jimmy," he said, using the name with familiarity and contempt. "It's time they paid for what they did to you. To us."

Smash-Mouth's response was a guttural growl. AJ understood the meaning behind it all too well. Their bond was forged in the fires of shared suffering and a mutual desire for revenge.

The shack pulsed with a sinister energy as AJ continued his preparations. He tested the weight of the barbed-wire-laden football, feeling its deadly potential. "They won't see it coming," he said softly, a dark smile spreading across his distemporally cracking face. "They think they're safe, hiding away in their little cabin. But we'll show them. We'll make them understand."

Smash-Mouth moved closer, his deformed features becoming more distinct in the dim light. His jaw hung at a freakish angle, the result of that brutal beating that had shattered it long ago. The sight of it filled AJ with a renewed sense of purpose. This was no longer just about revenge. It was about justice. About making things right.

As the candle flickered and the shadows slithered, the two figures stood in silent communion, bound by their shared history and grim resolve. The shack, a relic of forgotten times, had become a crucible for their dark ambitions, where past and present converged in a deadly pact.

Outside, the wind howled through the trees as if the elements themselves warned of the impending storm. But inside the shack, there was only the steady, unrelenting rhythm of preparation, the calm before the tempest of retribution that was about to be unleashed.

CHAPTER 4: A PASSAGE TO INDICIA

Except for the Pinnacle Caves—and they are twenty miles off—the woods of Shadow Pine typically present nothing extraordinary. Oblivious to the horrors lurking nearby in these woods, Nancy's car journeyed to its destination. The cabin stood regally amidst the curves of the forest. In the heart of that wilderness, where trees told secrets to one another in the wind and the mountains stood as silent guardians of time, Nancy's car pulled to a gentle stop. She exited the car and found herself dwarfed by an imposing mountain cabin that stood tall, like an old watchman amidst nature's serenity. With the heaviness of nostalgia pressing down on her chest, Nancy hesitated, drinking in the scenery. Here, where civilization seemed but a distant memory, the air carried a silence, pierced only by the distant call of a night creature. The subtle chill of a mountain breeze, laced with the scent of pine and old memories, played with her hair, offering a transient comfort. The grandeur of the cabin, juxtaposed against the wild unknown, beckoned her inside, promising safety on a night that was yet to unveil its secrets.

Deep within the warmly lit confines of the cabin, Mary caught the familiar but once believed to be forgotten, sight of Nancy. "Nancy's here!" she announced, her voice reverberating with the timbre of times gone by.

Shelly animatedly hastened to the door. As it creaked open, it revealed a momentarily paused Nancy clutching her tattered suitcase. "Nancy! I am so glad you could make it. It's so good to see you! Come in," beckoned Shelly.

Joining the welcoming chorus, Deborah chimed in with her gentle cadence, "Hi, Nancy." At the same time, from her position on a worn-out armchair, Linda gave a silent yet heartfelt wave.

Mary, her eyes sparkling with vindication, marveled at Nancy's appearance. "You look great! Just how I remember you!" she remarked, awash with warmth.

Nancy uncomfortably returned the compliment, "You look great, too."

It seemed Nancy's arrival had validated a secret belief Mary held. "See," she noted to Deb with a hint of pride.

Amidst this wave of emotions, Deborah drew Nancy into a tender embrace. "It's really nice to be here with you, Nancy. We've missed you, and we appreciate you coming to spend the weekend with us," she murmured.

Deborah's genuine and warm embrace was incongruous with Shelly's rehearsed hospitality. In her facile tone, she proffered, "Nancy, make yourself at home. There's plenty of room to spread out. Your bedroom is upstairs on the right. The kitchen down here is fully stocked if you're hungry. Can I get you a drink? Wine? Something stronger?"

"Just some water would be fine," Nancy requested with reticence.

"Linda, go get Nancy some water!" Shelly snapped.

Linda took on the task, albeit slightly reluctantly. Deborah gently took Nancy's suitcase, "And I'll show you to your room!"

Nancy moved slowly enough that Linda could hurry back with water in hand. However, even in this cocoon of warmth and nostalgia, Nancy's hands trembled slightly as she accepted the glass from Linda. She took a sip. The water failed to wash away the uncertainty that clouded her eyes. Deborah and Nancy walked off.

Mary leaned back into a plush, faded armchair. Her face, illuminated by the soft glow of a nearby lamp, wore a satisfied expression. "I think that went really well," she mused.

Shelly glanced around the room, already visualizing the scene she wanted to create. "Linda, let's get the living room set up for later," she directed with a tone that brooked no argument.

But the unknown lurked outside, where the mischance flirted with the staunch moonshine. A pair of eyes bore into the cabin from the veil of shadows, watching the reunion unfold with unwavering intensity. An undercurrent of tension threaded through the narrative, promising that this was the beginning and the winter night would be extended.

CHAPTER 5: REMEMBRANCE OF THIEVES PAST

For a long time, Nancy used to go to bed early. The sooner she got to the nightmares, the sooner they might end for the night. Guided by Deborah's attempt at being a reassuring influence, Nancy ascended the staircase to find solace in her temporary quarters. The stairs creaked under their weight, each step a reminder of the passage of time. Out of her element, she moved into her new sleeping quarters with a feigned enthusiasm.

Her room was small but cozy, with a large window that offered a breathtaking view of the forest. The bed, covered in a handmade quilt, invited her to rest. Deborah placed the suitcase by the foot of the bed and turned to Nancy with a warm smile.

Nancy sat on the edge of the bed, her fingers tracing the patterns on the quilt. The room felt like maybe it could serve as a haven where she could temporarily escape the ghosts of her past. Yet, despite the warmth and comfort, a sense of unease lingered.

Nancy gazed out at the moonlit landscape, her reflection merging with the abyss beyond the glass. She couldn't shake the feeling that they were not alone, that the past was not as far behind them as they wished to believe.

Deborah sought an intimate moment with her old friend. The warm ambient lighting painted the room in hues of soft gold, giving the entire space a dreamlike quality that complemented the fantastic reality Nancy faced. In the 15 years squandered since high school, she never once believed she might see her former friends again. Nancy had made no progress toward shedding the disconnect between the victory and the pains of the day she stopped Angela from continuing her bloodthirsty spree.

Overhead, a worn-out ceiling fan rotated lazily, barely making a sound yet providing a comforting rhythm to the room. But this comfort could not calm Nancy's unease. What if the fan were to become dislodged? Could it cause her harm, or worse yet, injure Deborah? Would Nancy be responsible for any calamities caused by luring Deborah into this hazardous space? Nancy knew logically the room was safe and that the fan was flimsy and light, unlike some of the other ornate fixtures in the cabin, but her thoughts and reality were rarely reconciled.

Nancy's eyes darted around the room, scanning for a justification to be on high alert, but found none. She sighed, resigned to a calmness that was more troubling to her than a justifiable fear. The two women faced each other. The import of years and unresolved tensions held like a wall between them. Deborah, her eyes glistening with sincerity and perhaps a touch of melancholy, opened the channel for reconciliation. "I know I said it already, but it's really great to see you," she murmured.

Nancy hesitated, searching for something to do with her hands. When she finally spoke, she quivered with uncertainty. "Thank you. It's great to see you all, too. I am just...was it a mistake for me to come here?"

Deborah leaned forward, her posture protective. "I know Shelly pressured you. She's not the nicest person."

A sigh escaped Nancy's lips, revealing an emotional tumult beneath. "I feel a little bit responsible for that."

Brushing a stray strand of hair behind her ear unassuredly, Deborah earnestly offered the best words of solace she could muster. "No, that's unreal. Don't let her convince you that you owe her anything."

As this conversation flowed, Nancy found herself drawn into the emotional current, her defenses gradually crumbling. "I know. I don't really," she admitted.

Deborah's eyes held an unmistakable spark of admiration. "You are a powerful woman. You stood up against impossible odds and came out on top. Bravery can have a high cost. I really admire you, Nancy."

Humbled, Nancy could only shake her head.

Undeterred, Deborah persisted. "I mean it. No one else will say it, but you saved all of our lives."

With a soft, introspective voice, Nancy countered, "I just did the only thing I could do."

Drawing a deep breath, Deborah laid bare her own vulnerabilities. "And I know you paid the price for that. I'm sorry I wasn't a very good friend at the time. We all got lost for a little while there. But I really think that's coming to an end. Mary's now," Deborah searched for a positive outcome among her friends, "Well, Linda…okay, Shelly," but the search was fruitless, and she came up short, finally admitting, "…maybe we're all a little stuck. Maybe we can help each other get our lives back."

The possibility hung in the air, and Nancy finally spoke, "Maybe."

Deborah's curiosity about the intervening years bubbled to the surface in the lull that followed. "What have you been up to for the last 15 years?"

Gazing distantly, as though accessing memories from another lifetime, Nancy responded, "Nothing, really."

Unconvinced, Deborah probed gently, "I'm sure you've been doing something."

Almost inaudibly, Nancy confessed, "Mostly thinking."

Recognizing the depth of this simple admission, Deborah nodded. "Thinking is important. I've been going to meetings down at the bookstore, a lot of women getting together and talking about the world. You can come with me sometime."

But the emotional roller-coaster had taken its toll on Nancy. "I might like to be alone for a few minutes," she murmured.

Deborah was hurt by Nancy's dismissal, but perhaps she had said too much and made her feelings for Nancy too evident. Deborah retraced the conversation to make sure she had not hinted about any of her more extreme years.

Like many, she had been caught up in the allure of the *SCUM Manifesto* and other radical works. She had even met with Valerie Solanas several times during her brief stint as a National Organization for Women resignee. Deborah, however, disagreed vehemently with Solanas's extension of the manifesto into the terrible act of shooting Andy Warhol.

This action fractured the movement. Some feminists felt that the destruction of any powerful man who used the beauty of women like Edie Sedgwick as a means to their own end and also mocked women by accepting men as women must be destroyed by any means. Others, including Deborah, viewed both issues differently, believing that Warhol, in particular, created equal opportunities for women and advanced the idea of womanhood by involving Candy Darling and others like her in his work. She also felt deeply moved by his *Shot Marilyns* and his questioning of the nature of art.

Deborah reflected on the subtle nuances of love and companionship that transcended traditional romance for the first time at a screening of Warhol's *Outer and Inner Space* at the Ypsilanti Film Archive. Her admiration for Edie Sedgwick made her consider other women in her life for whom she felt similarly.

She had discovered then that the affection she felt for Nancy was more than mere friendship. Her heart had always raced faster when she was with Nancy, and she longed for moments alone with her. Those late-night talks and shared secrets had meant more to Deborah than either of them had ever realized.

The books Deborah read about women living outside the oppressive hold of men also opened her eyes to the possibility that her feelings were not just figments of her imagination. She had accepted this part of herself, yet fearing rejection kept her from expressing it openly. Now, as she stood in the soft glow of Nancy's bedside lamp, her unspoken words hung heavily between them.

Respecting the boundaries Nancy had set when she requested time alone, Deborah rose gracefully. "I understand. Come down when you're ready."

In the room's stillness, punctuated only by the gentle hum of that ceiling fan, Nancy remained motionless for a long moment. A fleeting shadow shot past the window. Her eyes shifted toward it, but the obsidian veil of the night kept its secrets. Only cold, silent emptiness stared back.

CHAPTER 6: THE HAUNTING OF SHEL HOUSE

No live organism can continue for long to exist sanely under conditions of absolute reality; even ghosts and apparitions are supposed, by some, to dream. Shelly's family cabin, not sane, stood by itself against its woods, holding darkness within; it had stood so for eighty years and might stand for eighty more. The cabin's main room, with its vaulted wooden ceilings and rustic charm, had undergone a metamorphosis since the day's onset. The long, oak serving table that dominated the center of the room was laden with a cornucopia of dishes—steaming platters of food, bowls of rich sauces and desserts, and delicate crystal glasses filled with crimson liquids. Although Christmas was still a week away, its imminence was felt, as the lamps and candelabras bathed a lightly trimmed tree with an inviting glow. The sticky smell of pine and the earthy aroma of wine created an atmosphere ripe for merriment.

Deborah, Linda, Mary, and Shelly, ensconced in the plush, cushioned chairs surrounding the table, were engrossed in conversation. Their laughter reverberated in the spacious cabin, each burst of joy punctuating stories from yesteryears, tales of mischief, heartbreak, and love. Old melodies from the record player somewhere in the background rang a bell of nostalgia through their reunion.

Mary stood up with a dark bottle of perfectly aged wine shimmering in her grip. She filled each glass with practiced elegance, the ruby-red liquid catching the light. Everything was planned and executed to perfection. The stage was set.

Raising her own glass, her eyes shimmering with emotion, Mary declared, "A toast is in order. To Shelly. Thanks for bringing us all together and for sharing this amazing cabin. Here's to the future and our friendship." There was a brief, reverent pause before the air was punctuated by the symphony of clinking glasses and the collective cheers of affirmation.

Shelly nodded gracefully, her cheeks flushed with the compliment and the warmth of the room. "Thanks," she murmured, brimming with emotion. "I'm happy to have you all in my life again and so happy we could have this weekend together. Let's all just have some fun. I think we deserve it."

The words promised warm revelry and a collection of hard-earned cherished memories. They raised their glasses once more, affirming their intent to let go of past resentments and enjoy the present. Whether this intention could hold, however, remained to be seen.

Ever the performer, Linda stood up and began an impromptu re-enactment of one of their high school pep rallies. She mimicked the cheerleaders' routines, her exaggerated movements and spirited cheers eliciting peals of laughter from the others. "Give me a D! Give me an O! Give me an N-N-E-R! What does that spell? Donner High!" she shouted, her chants ricocheting off the walls.

Amidst this tableau of joy and celebration, an almost ethereal being descended the wooden staircase. The legendary Nancy, her frail form framed by the soft light from above, appeared. Her steps were tentative, her smile fragile, and her eyes sunken. She stood for a moment, an observer of the joyous scene, unseen and unheard, lost in the shadows of the past. This was not revelry for which she felt deserving. She could only imagine that her invitation was a mistake or, worse, a humiliation rite for which she served only as the victim. She considered other options but continued her descent into the belly of the jolly beast.

CHAPTER 7: LOOK BACKWARD, ANGEL

Naked and alone, they came into exile. As night draped its velvet cloak over the cabin, the women, now nestled in the embrace of the living room, stared at artifacts of a former life strewn atop the polished table surface—old photo albums with worn edges and fragile pages that betrayed secrets from their youth. Each image told a story, a fragment of time suspended forever. The centerpiece of this arrangement was the Donner High yearbook for their class. Nancy thought all of the copies had been destroyed by pact, but this one somehow remained.

The room flickered with the amber fulgurations of the grand stone fireplace, its flames cavorting while casting a reassuring mingling of light and shadow upon the walls. For this moment, these antitheses were unified in a choreographed balance. In fact, those elegant, wispy guardians, the scent of burning wood, and the delicate aroma of emptied bottles were all unexpected environmental perfections to the women. Even Nancy could not deny the meticulousness with which this meeting had been staged.

Lifting an album closer, Mary revealed an open page showcasing a collection of images from their cheerleading days. In their vibrant uniforms and youthful exuberance, the squad smiled back at them from the annals of history.

Mary, her eyes twinkling with mischief, pointed to one particular photograph. "I forgot her name, but she didn't last long on the squad. Thought she could come to a pep rally with no underwear. Seriously, who does that?"

With a knowing smile, Linda quipped, "You did that once."

Mary, feigning outrage, leaned back and laughed. "That's a long story!"

Linda's eyes gleamed with playful innuendo, "How long?"

Mary replied with a faux dramatic sigh, rolling her eyes, "Oh, stop."

Unable to resist joining, Shelly interjected amusedly, "I can't believe you brought the yearbook! I thought we all agreed to burn them."

Mary gently stroked the album's cover wistfully, "My mom bought another copy so she could always remember how beautiful we all were. I'm glad she did. Look how foxy we are in our uniforms!"

Deborah, the realist among them, wrinkled her nose in gentle disdain. "You'll never catch me in a skirt again."

Yet, amidst the joyful reminiscing, Linda's gaze turned inward, the edges of her eyes softened by memories. "We had our whole lives ahead of us."

Shelly wished to inject optimism to counter the sorrow and regret. She had a talent for this, albeit often rooted in a platitudinous cover of the hippie movement. Shelly gently nudged her friend, "We still do."

It was then that Nancy, reserved and reflective, surprised the group. Her lips curved into a genuine smile, her eyes misty with memories. The change in her demeanor was so stark that it captured everyone's attention.

"Nancy, are you...smiling?" Linda inquired, disbelief evident.

The ripple of astonishment swept through them as they all turned their gazes to Nancy. Her blush deepening, Nancy pointed at a particular photograph,

"Steve Tramer. One of the good ones. I haven't thought about him in years."

Linda's curiosity was insatiable, "I wonder what he's up to now!"

However, the bittersweet pang of reality intruded upon their reverie. Linda's face paled as the memory resurfaced and the jovial atmosphere soured. The other women exchanged glances, their joy dimming.

"Linda!" Shelly's voice was gentle yet laden with sorrow.

Feeling the gravity of her oversight, Linda's voice trembled with regret, "Oh, no. Sorry. I...I forgot."

A heavy silence blanketed the room, broken only by Linda's sheepish addition, "May he rest in peace."

CHAPTER 8: BLOOD RITUALS IN THE DARK

He came out of the shadows of the shack with his head lowered, ignoring the artifacts of mort hanging and twirling like a mobile that pressed around him and leaving it to them to steer out of his way. The feeble luminescence of a single red bulb did little to dispel the enveloping dark inside this desolate structure in the woods. The eerie, elongated outlines of blood dripping from severed limbs and stripped bones danced upon the mildewed walls. Every corner, every crevice, harbored secrets of its own. The stench of decay and old blood was overpowering, a nauseating blend that clung to the back of the throat and filled the lungs with each breath. The very air held the legacy of the horrors that had transpired within these walls and the suffusions of the acts of evil that migrated with its inhabitants.

Amidst this backdrop, a typically innocuous domestic act took on a sinister quality. With its off-white exterior dulled by age and use, a blender stood prominently on a table, bearing witness to and some responsibility for deeds it never intended. The countertop around it was littered with baleful tools: bloodstained knives, a rusty hacksaw, and a collection of jars filled with nameless substances. A grimy rag, stained with memories and cries perhaps best left buried, was being used to scrub the appliance's glass pitcher with an intensity bordering on fervor. Each swipe was accompanied by heavy, labored breaths that saturated the confined space, creating a rhythm of sinister determination.

The freshly cleaned but still streaky pitcher was returned to its throne and filled with a dark mush of blood and tissue. The foul concoction was a reminder of the grisly experiments that had taken place, a vile mockery of what the blender was designed to do. The device was activated, and the blades tore through the awful mixture, body morsels thrown against the glass with centrifugal force, visibly telling a new odious and nauseating tale with every rotation. The blender whirred, not with the soft hum of domesticity but with a heightened, ominous resonance, whistling to summon an unseen malevolence.

The noise of the blender was almost deafening in the small shack, drowning out the subtle creaks and groans of the old wooden structure. Now more uniformly pureed, the viscous, dark liquid splashed homogenously against the sides of the pitcher, and the room filled with the sickly sweet scent of fresh blood. Obliteration of the human form was a ritual of sorts, a dark homage to the corrupt minds that had conceived it.

Two figures shifted their forms into the light. AJ, a man of mysterious intent, had eyes that held tales of countless confrontations and countless humiliations that would no longer be tolerated. Smash-Mouth, his equally enigmatic counterpart, prepared for what lay ahead.

Smash-Mouth was a hulking figure who exuded an aura of menace. His deformed jaw, a dreadful physical manifestation of the violence he had endured, hung slightly ajar, giving him a perpetual look of spiteful hunger. His eyes, dark and unreadable, were fixed on the whirring blades, lost in thoughts only he could fathom. He reached up with one massive hand, brushing away the strands of oily hair that fell across his scarred face, revealing a patchwork of old wounds and fresh bruises.

Smash-Mouth's face resembled a mask. His maloculus skin, frozen to his paralytic mandible, had a festering agedness and a smoothness owing to its sopping lack of motility. Clotted slaver oozed from his maw. Besides consuming the rotten spoils of this private war, Smash-Mouth no longer bothered to swallow and slabbered continuously, glazing the bisqued attire from his younger days, which had become one with his flesh. The Donner High team's jersey was originally yellow, hiding much of the discoloration of time and salivary acridity. None of the pep squad would have been able to smile after the site of what the team colors had become.

While Smash-Mouth suffered this costume-like deformity and adopted this passively constructed filth, AJ's once handsome face had also become an abhorrent visage of grim determination, the lines deep from years of hardship and anger. His hands, calloused and scarred, moved with a precise efficiency as he adjusted the settings on the blender, ensuring the mixture's texture and density were just right.

The shack, an inherently indifferent structure, became an unwitting participant in the unfolding drama set to alter the course of the intertwined destinies between this pair and the nearby women. The walls, stained and splintered, seemed to absorb the tension in the air, amplifying the sense of impending doom.

Outside, the wind howled through the trees, its mournful cries blending with the mechanical whine of the blender, creating an unsettlingly outlandish symphony of horrors.

AJ shut off the blender and poured the contents into a series of small, clear jars. He screwed the lids on tightly, his hands steady despite the squalid task. Each jar was a piece of their plan, a step toward the retribution they sought. He lined them up neatly on the table, his eyes gleaming with a wicked satisfaction.

Smash-Mouth's musings were a whirlwind of fury and melancholy, a chaotic maze in his demented mind. Recollections of the degradation he suffered at the hands of the Donner High football team replayed ceaselessly, stoking his unquenchable thirst for retribution. Each monstrous reflection of his disfigured countenance in the blood-splattered blender pitcher only intensified his resolve. He had morphed into the very nightmare they had always called him, the nightmare manifested first by his mother and now inherited. He was determined to make them confront the absolute terror they had wrought.

AJ was driven by a different kind of cold-bloodedness. His rage was a cold, methodical force honed by years of silent suffering and meticulous plotting. He had been Jimmy's sole ally, the one who had seen the potential in his friend when others only saw a monstrosity. AJ's thoughts were a detailed blueprint for vengeance, each step carefully orchestrated to inflict the maximum psychological and physical anguish on their oppressors. The sight of the blood-filled jars arrayed on the table elicited a sinister smile; they were emblems of his dominance, his command over the situation, and his ability to reverse their fortunes.

Smash-Mouth's gaze lingered on AJ, a mix of reverence and trepidation in his eyes. Despite his monstrous exterior, a part of him recognized AJ's brilliance and his ruthless efficiency. It was AJ who had masterminded their campaign, molding Smash-Mouth's raw fury into a precise instrument of retribution. Smash-Mouth trusted AJ implicitly, knowing that together, they were an invincible force, bonded by their shared history and unbreakable loyalty.

Smash-Mouth's thoughts wandered to the moment their paths first intersected. He remembered the din of the locker room, the stench of sweat and dread as the football team closed in on him. AJ had emerged from nowhere, a guardian angel wrapped in shadows, pulling him from the brink. That night had sealed their fates, setting them on a trajectory that culminated in this moment of imminent vengeance.

AJ's thoughts were precision-focused on the logistics of their plan. He had spent countless hours meticulously preparing for this night, anticipating every possible scenario. His mind was a fortress of strategy and foresight, unassailable and unwavering. As he looked at Smash-Mouth, a surge of pride swelled within him. His friend, once shattered and cast aside, was now a formidable force, a corollary of AJ's unwavering faith.

The two were an unholy alliance, a symbiotic partnership forged in pain and vengeance. Smash-Mouth's brute strength complemented AJ's shrewd intellect, creating a tempest of destruction. Together, they had devised a plan that was as much a psychological assault as it was a physical one. The jars of blood were just the overture, a prelude to the horrors they would unleash on their unsuspecting victims.

As they looked out through the window into the night, their thoughts converged on the same singular purpose—to make their enemies suffer, to reclaim the power that had been stripped from them. The forest seemed to come alive around them, the swaying trees presenting their silent vows of vengeance. Smash-

Mouth's hulking form moved with a predator's grace while AJ's eyes gleamed with anticipation.

The night was theirs, and they would stop at nothing to see their dark vision realized.

"Everything is ready," AJ said, his voice low and filled with a dark promise.

Smash-Mouth nodded, a guttural sound escaping his throat. It was a sound of agreement, of readiness. He picked up one of the jars, examining it closely. He moved with a deliberate slowness.

The shack's door creaked open, and the cold night air rushed in, carrying the scent of pine and earth. AJ and Smash-Mouth stepped out, the moon casting a pale light on their retreating forms. The thick seemed to close around them.

As they disappeared into the night, the shack stood staid once more, a silent synecdoche of the horrors conceived within its walls. The red bulb flickered one last time before burning out, plunging the shack into darkness, leaving behind only the fading ripples of its lurid history. The stage was set, the players were ready, and the night was far from over.

CHAPTER 9: THE GHOST OF THE PAST

The sun had already set, and the night's fingers enveloped the trees. Back in Shelly's family retreat, the reunion continued. Mary delicately seated herself beside Nancy, those yellowed photo albums still open before them. Mary's fingers trailed across the black and white images as emotions rose. The fire crackled softly, adding a warm, comforting soundtrack to the nostalgic atmosphere.

"These are like staring at ghosts," Mary cracked, heavy with emotion. The photos seemed to shimmer under her touch as if the memories they held were eager to be released into the present.

Deborah, always the sensitive one, took a deep breath before responding, "Yeah," laden with the weight of their shared past.

Mary, her eyes rimmed with tears, felt a pang of regret. "I'm sorry. I thought these would help lighten the mood. Things have felt so heavy for years. I miss the glory days!" Her fingers traced the outline of a photograph, her mind drifting back to simpler times.

From across the room, with the glow of the table lamp illuminating her features, Shelly attempted to soothe the mood, a steady anchor in the emotional storm, "It's okay, Mary. It's part of the healing journey we're on."

Nancy, her ordinarily stoic face softened by the memories, carefully lifted a photograph. It was a group shot, smiles frozen in time. "I like this one," she murmured, pausing before nostalgically adding, "We were happy then."

Lost in the sea of faces, Shelly's sharp eyes picked out one in particular. "There's Jimmy Smazmoth. Before the incident." Her tone was flat, almost clinical, as if discussing a distant event populated with strangers rather than something that had deeply affected them all.

Nancy, her brow furrowed, questioned, "Incident?"

Deborah, always one to weigh her words, remarked, "That's one way to put it."

Shelly leaned in conspiratorially, "Well..." She let the word hang in the air, inviting curiosity and dread.

Interest now piqued, Nancy's voice held a tremble, "Does that justify beating him?" Her eyes widened.

Shelly's bitterness bubbled up. "Do you still have a thing for him? I remember his mom, Angela, kept trying to fix you two up." Her words were pointed and tinged with resentment.

But Nancy ignored Shelly's barb. She was not to be derailed. Shelly pushed the knife deeper. "Before you stabbed her, of course."

Shelly then went a step further, and certainly too far, making disturbing imitations of Angela dying. Linda interjected, sensing the need for levity, "I tutored him once. Not exactly by choice. Angela kind of forced me by offering money." Her tone was light, trying to defuse the tension.

Deborah, her gaze unwavering, said, "It's honest work! Women need to be able to support themselves. You met him at the library, I'm hoping?"

Linda, her memories still vivid, clarified in a reluctant tone, "His house."

Mary's eyes widened with curiosity. "Wow."

Linda continued to paint a picture. "I remember a musty smell. It was quiet. Almost too quiet. I heard the clock ticking." Her words conjured vivid images of a house filled with silence and tension.

Amidst the gravity, Shelly, true to form, leaked hatred. "Cuckoo. Cuckoo." Her voice was mocking, cruel.

Reliving the moment, Linda recalled, "Jimmy was always staring." She leaned forward, her eyes wide and unblinking, imitating the stare that had once unsettled her. "Angela brought out these peanut butter and jelly sandwiches, but the bread was kind of moldy."

Mary's face scrunched in disgust, voice filled with genuine revulsion, "Yikes."

Linda's voice held a shiver, "I just felt uncomfortable there." Her words were a confession, a release of long-held unease.

Curiosity evident, Deborah asked, "I'll bet. What happened?"

Eager to share her hasty exit, Linda smirked triumphantly, proud of her quick thinking, "I faked a headache or maybe the plague and got the hell out of there."

Mary and Deborah, visualizing the scene, burst into a fit of laughter as Linda continued, "I don't think she ever forgave me," she confessed. At least the secrecy of this memory was no longer a burden, even if the shame would forever be.

Mary, always protective of her friends, argued, "For what? You didn't do anything."

With a sigh, Linda explained, "Jimmy's grades slipped, and he almost got kicked off the football team." Her tone implied her guilt.

Deborah quickly comforted, "Oh, but that's not your fault. There could be a lot of reasons for that. The bullying, his weird mom...I guess she was doing her best. It's not on you, Linda."

Mary, with a contemplative expression, made an admission. "Well, since we're all sharing," she began, betraying a hint of hesitation, "Jimmy did ask me out once, but I turned him down."

Shelly's dark eyes widened, an expression of unfeigned surprise sweeping her features. "I didn't know that."

Mary's voice grew even softer. "Angela offered me money to go out with him."

Without missing a beat, Deborah joked, "It's honest work! Women need to be able to support themselves."

With a curious and playful glint in her eyes, Linda leaned forward. "Yeah, how was it?"

Mary's quick look toward Deborah held a dash of reproach. "I said no, of course. I had a reputation to protect."

Shelly's chuckle was followed by a playful barb. "And a very high opinion of yourself."

The room's atmosphere grew momentarily darker as Shelly mused, "Maybe if you had given him a chance, Angela wouldn't have killed the whole football team, blended them up, and fed them to him."

Nancy, visibly uncomfortable, shifted in her seat.

Hoping to bring the conversation back to safer ground, Mary added with a dash of introspection, "I probably could've handled it better. I could've handled a lot of things better. But I've grown."

Her brow arched in mischief and insinuation, Shelly redirected the conversation toward Deborah. "Deborah, what about you? Did his mother pay you to improve his running game?"

Deborah's graceful fingers tapped a silent rhythm on her armrest. "I tried to ignore all those players, but everyone on the team used to talk shit about Jimmy incessantly."

Shelly added her perspective. "Yeah, your nose was always in a book, and even you noticed how much the whole team couldn't stand Jimmy."

Deborah brushed it off as typical behavior. "That's just how guys are."

Nodding in agreement, Mary's gaze traveled toward the tree. "I tuned a lot of that stuff out. Guys gossiping can be such a turn-off."

The room was filled with the rich timbre of shared laughter. Linda, her cheek tinted with a slight blush, ventured her own secret, "Anyway, one day, out of sheer boredom, I just told a few people that I heard he had a big...well, you know."

Their laughter bubbled over once more.

"Whoa! You started that rumor?" Mary inquired, tinged with amusement.

Shelly's chuckle was more of a surprised gasp this time. "What?"

Linda, her posture more relaxed now, shared, "I thought it would help him. Maybe make him more popular. I didn't think it would inspire the ruthless, jealous wrath of his teammates."

Deborah opined, "Men are animals."

Mary, the perpetual gossip, jumped back in. "Hey, Shelly, didn't your sister have a crush on Jimmy? Or was it AJ? Remember AJ, they were always together?"

Linda soured. "Another one prone to staring." Her face contorted into a comical expression that transported them all back into a time of schoolyard tales and teenage exploits.

"I've never really talked about this before," Shelly admitted. The vulnerability in her eyes was impossible to miss, at odds with her usually playful demeanor. "Brenda had a secret crush at school. At first, I assumed it was AJ."

The social cost of the revelation was apparent. The subtle rustle of fabric and the distant chirping of crickets from outside were the only sounds that punctuated the silence.

Shelly continued sharply, "But I found one of her notebooks, and it had Brenda Smazmoth written all over it."

"Wow," Linda managed to utter.

"No way," Mary added, her fingers playing absently with the hem of her dress.

Shelly, her gaze distant, continued her tale. "I know. I'm not sure if he felt the same in return. I guess we'll never know."

Shelly's gaze locked onto Nancy, her words deliberate and heavy with implication. "I know he definitely carried a torch for you."

Nancy, with her gentle demeanor and modest attire, went blank. Her cheeks flushed, and her eyes, usually so confident, darted around the room.

Unyielding, Shelly pressed on, "Of course, everyone loves Nancy."

The tension of those words was palpable. Shelly sipped her wine, the crimson liquid seeming to deepen in color in response to the unfolding drama. As she placed the glass back on the coaster, the stillness in the room was stifling. Nancy shifted uneasily in her chair, the golden brocade patterns shimmering as if sharing her discomfort.

Nancy was a teetotaller but had little philosophical commonality with Carrie Nation. Abstinence was a choice she made with unwavering conviction. Unlike the others who sought solace or celebration in the occasional drink, Nancy eschewed alcohol altogether. Her decision was not borne out of disdain for spirits but rather from a deep-seated need to always remain vigilant. The events of her past had taught her the brutal lesson that danger could lurk in the most unexpected places, and she couldn't afford to let her guard down, even for a moment.

The harrowing memories of Angela Smazmoth's murderous rampage were baked into her mind. Nancy knew that her sharpness and alertness were her greatest allies in facing whatever threats might emerge. Alcohol, she believed, dulled the senses and clouded judgment, luxuries she couldn't afford in her perpetual state of high alert.

She imagined her friends might tease her for her abstinence, so she left things at quiet declination. Nancy feared that her resemblance to Sally Field was already enough to earn a nun nickname, which was highly undesirable given her dislike of organized religion. To add temperance to the mix would undoubtedly doom her to that path. Thus, lacking this knowledge, the women continued offering Nancy drinks and urging her to relax. But her resolve never wavered. Her sobriety was her shield, a constant reminder of the vigilance required to protect herself and those she cared about from the ever-present shadows of her past.

There was one way in which Nancy's views resembled those of Hatchet Granny. While Nancy preferred to destroy perceived danger with a blade rather than a hatchet, they both had a willingness to take matters into their own hands. Perhaps someday, high schools around the country, or at least the region, might deck their halls with banners proclaiming, "All Nations Welcome But Nancy."

Not even Deb knew what to say to break the tension. All those courses in de-escalation and negotiation she took at the women's center were no match for the awkward travails of reality.

Nancy rose from her seat and made her way to one of the large windows, which offered a breathtaking view of the mountains. She pressed her face against it. The cool glass touching her forehead was a welcome distraction from the intensity of the room and a juxtaposition to the warmth of the proximal crackling flames just beyond the hearth.

Close on her heels, Mary, with an empathetic furrow to her brow, followed her, an air of genuine concern surrounding her. The soft glow from the fireplace reflected in her eyes, and it was evident that she was deeply attuned to the emotional turmoil Nancy was experiencing.

Drawing closer, Mary reached out, her fingers gently brushing Nancy's shoulder, grounding her with a touch as much an inquiry as a source of comfort. "Hey, are you okay?" she softly murmured.

Nancy hesitated momentarily. "Yeah. It's been a while since I've been able to relax. I'm not sure how to let go."

Mary found a way to make the most superficial statements profound in the moment. She offered her simple wisdom, "It takes time. That's why we're here. If you need to cry, cry. If you want to laugh, laugh."

There was a brief pause, the kind that often precedes a vulnerable revelation. "If I want to scream?" Nancy inquired.

With a glint of mischief in her eyes, Mary countered with playful humor, "Plenty of open space out here. I'll join you. No one would hear us scream for miles."

A small smile graced Nancy's lips, a subtle disclosure of the comfort she derived from Mary's words. Neither realized the portending implications of their isolation. The distinctive timbre of Shelly's voice beckoned from across the room, breaking the ease of this moment of connection. "Hey, it's Angela."

Mary's eyebrows knit together in confusion. She hastened to the plush couch, joining Shelly and Linda, who were engrossed in flipping through the yearbook. Nancy lingered by the window, the vestiges of her contemplation still clouding her gaze.

A candid snapshot captured the attention of all present. It depicted the group's younger selves, brimming with jubilation, but an eerie juxtaposition was evident. Angela Smazmoth lurked in the background, her countenance a study in animosity.

"I never noticed her there before," Mary observed.

Deborah chimed in, staking a claim to the sentiment everyone already felt, "She's certainly shooting daggers at us back there."

Not one to let the mood turn somber, Mary lightened the air with her sardonic wit, "If looks could kill," she quipped, stopping before walking the cliche to its noxious conclusion, "I'll just cut her out of that one."

Linda's body pulsed with a distinct chill, "Yeah. Bad juju. I can feel it."

Finally roused from her introspection, Nancy approached, eyes narrowing on Angela's malevolent stare in the photograph. Recognizing the collective discomfort, Shelly took it upon herself to snap the album shut, punctuating the end of the unsettling interlude.

An awkward silence overtook the women. Outside, as the night deepened, the world outside the cabin seemed to settle into a similar hush. The muted calls of distant creatures occasionally punctuated this profound quiet, but mainly, the absence of life and sound seized the impression.

How long could this silence hold?

CHAPTER 10: NANCY

Last night, she dreamt she went to Donner High again. Tonight, Nancy, long retreated to her room feeling proud of her bravery and the day's achievements, now lay sleeping. Though ostensibly at rest, her sleep was a tempestuous journey through the landscapes of her subconscious. Her lithe frame writhed, and her eyes, hidden beneath delicate lids, darted back and forth in a frantic dance.

Dreams intertwined with memories, each image a ghostly reminder of the past she could never entirely escape. The truth distorted in this mélange of portentous and petrifying realities.

Shadows of faces she once knew flickered, their eyes hollow, their mouths contorted into screams she could not hear. The corridors of her mind became a winding, spinning labyrinth, each turn leading her deeper into melancholia.

She stood in an endless, desolate field, the ground beneath her feet cracked and dry, stretching infinitely into the horizon. The sky above massed in ominous clouds, their roiling depths occasionally illuminated by flashes of distant lightning. Each bolt revealed fleeting glimpses of twisted trees, their branches reaching out like skeletal fingers, clawing at the air in silent torment.

As she wandered through this forsaken landscape, the air coagulated with an oppressive density, making each breath a struggle. She felt an inexplicable pull, drawing her toward a shadowy figure in the distance. The figure remained indistinct as she approached, shrouded in a veil of gloom that seemed to absorb the light around it. Despite her growing dread, she felt compelled to move closer, her steps slow and hesitant.

The ground beneath her began to shift, the cracks widening into deep chasms that threatened to swallow her whole. She teetered on the edge, her heart pounding as she tried to maintain her balance. From the depths of these abysses, she could hear a low, mournful wail reverberating through her bones and filling her with an all-encompassing fear.

Suddenly, she was back in her childhood home, the walls and furniture warped and distorted as if viewed through a funhouse mirror. The once-familiar rooms were now alien and menacing, the colors muted and walls emitting a rancid smell. She wandered through the hallways, the doors lining them closed tight, their surfaces marred by deep gouges and scratches.

She reached out to touch one of the doors, and as her fingers brushed the wood, it swung open with a creak, revealing an inky void. From within, tendrils of darkness snaked out, wrapping around her wrists and ankles. She struggled against the pull, but the more she fought, the tighter the grasp became, constricting her movements and filling her with a paralyzing terror.

In the depths, she saw glimpses of her own reflection, distorted and fragmented, her face bent into expressions of anguish and agony. Her own eyes stared back at her, empty and devoid of hope. She felt herself sinking deeper into the void.

As this Ephialtian vision ate at her soul, the outside glow filtered through her bedroom curtains, playing tricks upon the ornate décor. Its light weaved fables of phantom silhouettes, mimicking the vivid images in Nancy's mind while the true phantoms turned a foul waltz nearby in the woods.

The intricate patterns on the wallpaper seemed to shift and move in a silvery glow, creating an ever-changing tapestry of light and shadow that made the room feel unsettlingly and yet gorgeously alive. The faint rustling of the curtains, stirred by an unseen breeze, wheezed as if the room itself was breathing, pulsing with an anima of its own.

Unprompted, the sturdy oak door of her chamber creaked open of its own volition. As it slowed to a halt and the creak subsided, it almost immediately slammed shut thunderously, shaking the house and rousing Nancy. She sat up, bewildered. Before she could fully comprehend this enigmatic sound, the door opened again, almost pointing a ghastly spectral finger at the disruption's haunted source.

A distant, persistent scratching from the hall beckoned her. Nancy should have been afraid, but the gossamer threads of reality remained frayed, and her emotions and instincts were tangled and malfunctioning. This hideous reality was undoubtedly no more objectionable than the wash of the persistent phantasmagorical vision, its dread subsiding while the lingering stain remained uncomfortably rebarbative.

Trancelike, she ventured forth to investigate, her bare feet silent on the cold wooden floor. She exited the room as if gliding. Her nightgown coursed and rippled in the drafts. Was it just the cooling, nocturnal air flow of a rustic, bucolic paradise, or could the rising mephitis of evil move the air about in such a manner?

Descending down the staircase toward the grandeur of the living room, Nancy's senses were assailed by the benign culprit of the scratching—an errant branch dancing with the whims of the wind against that pane of glass she had earlier gazed through toward the majestic mountains. The relief that washed over her was palpable, but it was short-lived. The cabin, now bathed in moonlight, seemed both familiar and alien, just like her childhood home felt in the dream. Every creak and groan was a reminder of its age and the secrets it held.

A methodical, rhythmic thud at her back broke the stillness. She turned. The sight was almost surreal. A football descended step by step.

THUMP!

THUMP!

THUMP!

As the ball settled at the base of the staircase, curiosity edged out Nancy's apprehension. She advanced, bending down to inspect the peculiar object. Yet, just as her fingers brushed its worn surface, a vice-like grip ensnared her wrist. Shocked, her gaze traveled upwards, only to be met with the jagged-toothed half grin of Smash-Mouth. His roar seemed to be birthed from the most bottomless pits of her nightmares. As the crescendo of her horror reached its zenith, she burst awake, safe in the bed she had just dreamed she had left.

Nancy's breathing was rapid, her skin glistening with a sheen of sweat. Her trembling fingers sought the comfort of light, illuminating her surroundings. The familiar room, with its cozy furnishings and warm hues, returned. Yet, the shadows in the corners seemed darker, more menacing. As her heart rate steadied, a profoundly unpleasant realization settled upon her. These reveries, though alarming, were becoming a hauntingly familiar part of her existence—a notion that troubled her deeply.

Could this be yet another dream within a dream, or was she now safe from all excepting the dangers of her tormented mind? She questioned the nature of her reality, the lines between dreams and wakefulness blurring in the aftermath of her frightful visions.

As she posed this question to herself, she was drawn inexorably to a specific corner of her room, her eyes fixed on a scene that was out of place—the looming silhouette of her closet, the innocuous presence of an old chair, and an enigmatic form, crowned with what appeared to be a helmet, nestled sinisterly behind. As if sensing her gaze, this ominous apparition seemed to retract, melting away from her line of sight.

Though she feared what might happen if she averted her gaze from the now empty corner, with a heart pounding in her chest, a desperate need for illumination drove Nancy to reach out. With a swift motion, the glow of her bedside lamp bathed the room. She whipped her head back to scan the nook. With the benefit of illumination, the chair and closet now seemed perfectly normal, but the fear lingered.

Summoning her courage, she disentangled herself from the confines of her bedding and treaded hesitantly toward the previously malevolent chair. Its velvet emptiness was a relief. She sighed, the tension in her shoulders easing slightly. She took several return steps toward the soft bed but stopped short of climbing in. What of that sinister closet? Could evil be hiding inside? She recalled her certainty as a child that the monsters under her bed would get her and the apparent foolishness of that childish worldview as she entered her teen years.

But as fate would have it, her views regressed as those imaginary monsters became real in those formative years. Now, she wasn't quite sure where her perspective landed.

She flung the closet open, expecting nothing, giving way to reflexive relief before she made a haunting discovery. Her eyes met a relic from another era—a dated football helmet like the Donner High football team wore just 15 years before.

The helmets were outdated even then, but the school clung to the strange tradition, disregarding the safety and comfort of its students. And while Jimmy Smazmoth's beating would not have been wholly shielded by more modern prophylactic headgear, more shock absorption and a metal face shield may have reduced the injury to something recuperable.

Unsettled but capable of explaining away the possible coincidence of the leather helmet in the closet, Nancy returned to her bed. She lay back down, pulling the covers up to her chin, her eyes scanning the room, searching for any other signs of disturbance.

As Nancy relaxed and settled into the bed, her breathing slowed. Yet, the fear lingered, a constant companion in the silence of the night. Nancy's thoughts drifted to the day's events, the reunion with her old friends, the shared memories, and the haunting peal of the past that seemed to shadow their every move. She wondered what the coming days would bring and whether they would find the closure they all so desperately needed.

As she lay there, the sound of the wind rustling through the trees outside lulled her back toward sleep. Nancy closed her eyes, hoping for a dreamless sleep but knowing that the phantoms of her past were never far away, especially in her subconscious. She knew that, like long forgotten memories rematerializing in a dream, the past is never truly gone. It lingers, waiting patiently for the right moment to resurface.

CHAPTER 11: THE UNEXPECTED GUEST

It was three minutes past eight. Under the flavescent sunlight and azure skies of a splendid day, Shelly, Mary, and Linda ventured into the lush woods, exploring one of the scenic nature trails. Amidst the vastness of nature, the trail carved its way through the woods, kissed by the gentle sun. The sky was crystal clear, and its hue mirrored the feeling of serenity in the woods. Shelly, Mary, and Linda shared this slice of peace. As they strolled along, their laughter and animated conversation lilted about in the tranquil air.

Mary raised a whimsical topic with a mischievous glint in her eye. "Do you remember that old fairy tale about leaving a trail of breadcrumbs to find your way back?" she asked.

Shelly responded with a playful grin, "Oh, it's sort of a wraparound trail. It's hard to get lost out here. The main road is just a few miles away if you need to get back to civilization—SHIT!"

Mary's expression shifted to solicitude. "What's wrong?"

Shelly pointed excitedly ahead to a peculiar shack nestled in the distant woods. "Look over there!"

Mary's realization was accompanied by a thoughtful nod. "Oh."

Still wearing a grin, Shelly commented, "I've been coming out here for years, and I've never seen that before."

Linda, who had caught up with them, was far less thrilled by the discovery. She stated resolutely, "I don't care to find out."

Shelly persisted. "Come on, where's your sense of adventure?"

Mary, however, remained steadfast. "I left that in the city. Come on, we should head back."

Nodding in agreement, Linda took the lead as they turned to retrace their steps, leaving the enigmatic shack behind. The path back seemed longer, their previous light-heartedness now tainted by unease. They walked without words, the only sound being the crunch of leaves underfoot.

Suddenly, a mysterious and unkempt backwoods hillbilly emerged from the dense woods, catching them off guard.

Mary, startled by his sudden appearance, exclaimed, "Jesus! Why are you sneaking up on us?"

The hillbilly remained nonchalant, seemingly oblivious to the startled reaction. "Lovely day out here, ain't it? Almost as lovely as you three."

As Mary and Shelly exchanged uneasy glances, Linda chose to look away, her discomfort apparent.

Shelly attempted to defuse the situation, stating, "Just passing through. Don't want any trouble."

The hillbilly, now sporting a suggestive smirk, continued to gaze at Mary, his breathing growing raspier, much to her discomfort. "You all are not from around here!" he inadvertently shouted, quickly realizing his delivery showed an enthusiasm that could be misconstrued as a threat.

Mary, growing defensive, responded, "No."

The hillbilly shifted his gaze to Shelly, hinting at his knowledge. "You are, though. Your family owns that cabin on the hill. You out here for long?"

Mary's defenses remained up, and her unease was palpable as the stranger's unsettling stare persisted.

Mary fabricated a story in an attempt to deter him. "We're scoping the land. We came to hunt...with guns. A lot of guns."

Linda, playing along, added, "And we've even got bullets!"

Shelly nudged Linda, signaling her to cease her embellishments. Linda, realizing her mistake, hung her head in embarrassment.

The hillbilly, still oblivious to the tension he'd created, persisted with his advances. "Maybe I can join you sometime."

An awkward silence settled upon the group.

The hillbilly, undeterred, continued, "Think on it. You know where to find me."

Mary, with a coy demeanor, quipped, "This nature trail? By that rock over there?"

Shelly, eager to escape the situation, urged, "We should get going."

Shelly turned to the hillbilly, offering a polite farewell, although her words lacked sincerity. "It was ni...um...It's been an experience. Bye now."

With that, the three women briskly walked away, distancing themselves from the unsettling stranger.

With a disgusted expression, Linda remarked quietly, though probably not quietly enough, "What a creep."

As they walked away, the hillbilly shouted a final warning, again misunderstanding his tone, "Be careful out there now. This place is full of freaks!"

CHAPTER 12: THE BROKEN DAWN

The cabin was very still. In the bathroom, Nancy stood before the sink, the cool water splashing onto her face, providing a momentary respite. Her gaze fixated on her own reflection in the mirror. The dark circles under her eyes told the story of restless nights and troubled dreams. She stared into her own eyes, searching for a semblance of peace amidst the turmoil that had been her constant companion.

Returning to her room, Nancy perched herself on the edge of her bed. Her eyes wandered to the chair positioned across the room, the same chair from her unsettling dream. The ornate patterns on the upholstery seemed to mock her, reminding her of the night's haunting visions. She closed her eyes and took a deep breath, trying to find solace in the silence surrounding her. The room felt simultaneously comforting and confining, a sanctum and a prison. The walls seemed to close in on her, amplifying her sense of isolation.

Just then, Deborah's voice broke the quietude, calling out to Nancy from the doorway with a plate of food in her hands. "Hey, Nancy," Deborah greeted her. "Good morning. How'd you sleep?" Deborah's visit was a welcome distraction from Nancy's troubled thoughts.

Nancy replied, her tone hinting at an underlying unease as if the words might shatter under her anxiety. "Fine. I have to get used to this quiet, though. My mind plays tricks at night, you know."

Deborah empathized, understanding the difficulty of adjusting to unfamiliar surroundings. "I hear ya. Hey, there's some breakfast downstairs if you're hungry." She offered a warm smile, hoping to ease Nancy's discomfort.

Grateful for the offer, Nancy nodded. "Thanks. Where is everyone?" She glanced toward the window, noting the bright morning light streaming in.

Deborah informed her, "Mary and Shelly went for a walk on one of the trails. I'm sure Linda's tagging along. Shelly didn't want to wake you. You seemed peaceful."

Nancy's response was muted, "Far from peaceful," she said without eye contact, speaking instead toward the homely bedspread.

Deborah didn't quite catch the full extent of Nancy's confession. "What?" She leaned in slightly.

Nancy clarified softly, "Bad dreams. The usual." She was filled with quiet resignation, as if she had accepted the nightmares as an unavoidable part of her life.

Deborah, aware of the pain that lingered within Nancy, offered her some guidance. "Give it time." She placed a comforting hand on Nancy's shoulder, offering support through her touch.

Nancy expressed her skepticism. "Time. Sure." She sighed, her breath shaky.

Deborah shared an insight from her own experiences. "Shelly was the same for a while after Brenda died."

Nancy probed. "Do you have nightmares?" Her eyes searched Deborah's, looking for answers.

Deborah admitted with candor, "Sure, everyone does." She nodded, her expression serious.

Nancy desperately sought some kind of wisdom. "How do you deal?"

Deborah offered her perspective. "I just know there are a lot of things to keep fighting for." Her words were steady, imbued with a quiet strength.

Nancy contemplated this advice, her gaze dropping to the floor as she weighed the possibilities ahead. The words resonated with her, offering a glimmer of hope in the mournfulness of her thoughts.

The two women sat in silence for a moment. Nancy took a deep breath, feeling a sense of calm beginning to settle over her.

"Thanks, Deborah," Nancy said softly, filled with gratitude. "I needed that."

Deborah smiled warmly. "Anytime. We're all here for each other." She squeezed Nancy's shoulder gently before standing up. "Come on, let's get you some breakfast."

Nancy nodded, "I'll be down in a few minutes."

The journey ahead would be difficult, but with friends like Deborah by her side, it would be a little easier. Nancy watched as Deborah left the room, the door closing softly behind her. She was alone again, the silence pressing in. Her thoughts began to spiral, the familiar anxiety creeping back in. The nightmares, the memories—they were always there, lurking just beneath the surface.

She lay back on the bed, staring up at the ceiling. The fan continued its lazy rotations, a monotonous hum that did little to soothe her racing mind. She closed her eyes, willing herself to find some semblance of peace. But the unbidden images kept coming.

In her mind's eye, she saw the blood, the horror of that night—Angela's evil face, the screams of her friends, the terror that had gripped her heart. She felt the weight of the knife in her hand, the sickening crunch as it pierced flesh. The memories were so vivid, so real, that she could almost smell the coppery tang of blood in the air.

"How do you deal?" she had asked Deborah. The answer had seemed so simple, but Nancy knew that her battle was far from over. The demons of the past were tenacious, and they clung to her, refusing to let go.

Nancy's thoughts turned to her friends. Mary, Shelly, Linda, and Deborah had all suffered in their own ways. They had all faced their own demons. But they had come together, seeking solace and healing. Could she find the strength to let go of the past and embrace the future?

With a determined resolve, Nancy sat up and swung her legs over the side of the bed. She wouldn't let the nightmares define her. She wouldn't let the past control her. She had a chance to heal and find peace, and she would take it.

She stood up and walked to the door, her steps steady and purposeful. She paused momentarily as she reached for the handle, taking one last look around the room. The shadows still lingered but didn't seem as menacing as before. She took a deep breath, opened the door, and stepped out into the light.

The promise of a new day brought the hope of a brighter future, and Nancy was determined to seize it.

CHAPTER 13: BREAKFAST AT SHELLY'S

Nancy was always driven away from places where she had lived too long, the houses and their neighborhoods. Despite inherent hostilities and complexities, Nancy descended the stairs toward the kitchen, her curiosity piqued by the prospect of breakfast. She was greeted by the warm aroma of pancakes and the comforting ambiance of the cozy kitchen. Upon noticing Nancy's arrival, Deborah quickly poured a refreshing glass of orange juice and plated some pancakes, bringing them to the table with a friendly smile.

"Some breakfast," Deborah said, placing the plate and glass before her.

"Thanks," Nancy replied, appreciating the gesture. Deborah walked off to get more food. Nancy picked up the butter knife and fork, ready to enjoy her meal. However, as her knife sliced into a fluffy pancake, her senses were suddenly assaulted by a disturbing vision.

The pancake's flesh tore open, blasting a crimson geyser. In her mind, Nancy was no longer in the cozy kitchen. She was back in a dark, foreboding place, facing Angela, who was cunningly disguised as Smash-Mouth. She could see the fear and hatred in Angela's eyes. As she plunged the knife into Angela's body, blood seeped ominously from the wounds, staining Nancy's hands and the floor around her.

The horrific image was so vivid, so real, that it left her momentarily paralyzed. The flashback was fleeting, but it left Nancy visibly shaken. She dropped the knife onto the floor, her eyes frozen as if she was not permitted to search for answers.

Observing Nancy's strange reaction from just beyond the Christmas tree around the corner, Deborah couldn't help but be troubled by the display, wondering what had triggered such a response.

Just then, the back door swung open into the kitchen. Shelly, Linda, and Mary returned from their walk engaged in conversation. Their chatter ceased abruptly as they laid eyes on a petrified Nancy.

Shelly, attempting to ascertain if everything was all right, inquired, "Oh, hey. Good morning?"

Mary chimed in with a more friendly greeting. "Morning, Nancy."

Nancy, slightly flustered by her recent experience, stammered a response. "H-hey."

Shelly's gaze fell upon the fallen knife, prompting her to probe further. "Everything okay?"

In an effort to divert the conversation, Nancy deflected, "How was your walk?"

Mary offered an intriguing summary. "Eventful."

Shelly added her perspective. "Yeah, don't go out on the trails alone. We just had a strange conversation with a furry hillbilly."

Deborah, ever the provocateur, couldn't resist a playful jab. "Sounds like just your type, Mary."

Not amused by the remark, Mary responded, "Deb, don't. Just don't. He was hairy but in all the wrong places."

The group shared a hearty laugh before Deborah seized a moment to talk privately with Shelly.

As they retreated to a quiet corner of the upstairs hallway, Linda attempted to eavesdrop on their conversation but couldn't quite catch their hushed words. The curiosity gnawed at her, but mostly because she was without option, she respected their privacy.

Shelly, clearly agitated, sought clarification from Deborah. "Are you serious?"

Deborah calmly relayed her observation. "It was like something came over her. She was completely lost in that moment. I think we need to be careful and supportive."

Shelly, still processing the information, nodded slowly. "I get it. But we can't ignore what's happened, either."

Deborah placed a hand on Shelly's shoulder. "We'll figure it out together. Just take it easy on her for now. She's dealing with a lot."

Shelly left it open to interpretation. "We'll see."

CHAPTER 14: A PLAN FOR LIVING DEAD

Life's complexities often necessitate a plan to navigate through its challenges. Sometimes, such an endeavor includes all of the players. Sometimes, there are those left in the dark. That darkness was about to be illuminated.

The evening had arrived quickly, as this was one of the shortest days of the year, and the cabin's living room was once again bathed in the warm, pulsing glow of the fireplace. Nancy stood in isolation, her thoughts swirling as she stared into the flames. The other women drank wine and relaxed, their laughter and conversation a comforting backdrop to the otherwise serene night. They flipped through magazines and the yearbook again, still reminiscing about days gone by.

With purpose, Shelly began speaking to Linda in front of Nancy, ensuring she would overhear. Linda wasn't adept at pretending this was a genuine conversation, and Nancy quickly picked up on their intention.

"I started coming out here on my own every year since...well, the troubles," Shelly said, her tone somber. "I figured further away from town, school, and the reminders might help me cope with all the loss."

Sensing the conversation's gravity, Linda responded with a simple, "Brenda?"

Shelly nodded, her eyes reflecting deep sorrow. "I just kept seeing her laying there in her own blood. The look of fear in her eyes as she knew she was dying. If only I had gotten to her sooner. If only..."

Nancy felt a surge of discomfort, her heart heavy with guilt. Tears welled up in her eyes, and she struggled to hold them back.

Shelly continued, "Things changed. My parents became distant. I don't think they ever forgave me."

Linda, puzzled, asked with disdain, "Forgave you?"

"I was supposed to take care of Brenda. Keep her safe. I failed," Shelly admitted, her voice cracking.

Nancy couldn't contain her emotions any longer and wiped away her tears. Deborah noticed Nancy's distress and walked over to comfort her.

Shelly, attempting to correct course a bit, added, "We're far away from anything that can hurt us except what's in our minds. We have to confront that. Guide each other to enlightenment."

Deborah, always practical, asked, "So what do we do? Talk it out? Sing folk songs?"

Shelly shook her head. "I had an idea, but I need you all to open your minds."

The women stared at her, curiosity and apprehension mingling in their expressions.

Shelly took a deep breath and said, "We should perform a séance."

Mary, unfamiliar with the term, asked, "A say-what?"

"A séance," Shelly repeated patiently.

Intrigued by the idea, Linda added, "Contacting the spirit world. Intriguing."

Mary turned to Shelly, skepticism in her eyes. "Do you have experience with this?"

"I used it to contact Brenda once," Shelly admitted, softening with the memory.

A chill ran through the group as they absorbed the implications of her words.

Deborah, unable to contain her curiosity, asked, "What happened? Were you able to reach her? Did she say anything?"

With a heartfelt grin, Shelly replied, "She misses us."

The women smiled sympathetically, feeling an uncertain sense of connection with their lost friend.

Shelly then dropped a bombshell. "When we were looking at the yearbook, I thought of one person who might be able to put our minds at ease."

The women waited in anticipation, their eyes fixed on Shelly.

"I want to contact Angela Smazmoth," Shelly firmly announced.

Nancy's face went blank, her emotions tumultuous with fear and unresolved guilt. The day, which had started with a healing potential, was now turning into the kind of thing Nancy had hoped to avoid on this trip.

CHAPTER 15: HAUNT OF MIRTH

Nancy paused in surprise. The dimly lit hallway of the cabin echoed with the intensity of the conversation between Nancy and Shelly. Shadows fell on the walls, cast by the indecisive light from the fireplace, as the tension between the two women reached a boiling point.

"Absolutely not, Shelly! Are you out of your mind?" Nancy's voice was a mixture of anger and fear, her eyes wide with emotion.

Shelly stood her ground, her expression resolute. "Confronting our shared trauma is a way to release all the negativity that's been clouding our minds all these years. I met this guru in Big Sur once and—"

Nancy cut her off. "I just don't think we should mess around with this stuff. It could be dangerous."

Shelly's eyes narrowed slightly, a hint of frustration creeping in, "She might not even respond. Not with all the skepticism on display."

Nancy's voice softened, but the fear was still evident. "What if she does?"

"If she does, maybe we can get some answers," Shelly replied, her tone earnest.

"Answers to what?" Nancy demanded, her brows furrowed in confusion.

"Why she committed the murders," Shelly said simply as if the answer was obvious.

Nancy shook her head, her hands trembling. "We don't need a séance to tell us that."

Shelly took a step closer, speaking gently but firmly. "You're scared, I get it. She can't hurt you. She can't hurt any of us. Not anymore. You saw to that."

Nancy's eyes filled with tears. "I'm not proud of killing Angela. It haunts me every day."

Shelly's expression softened, her eyes filled with understanding. "Of course. Taking a life is not something you can just deal with. It was self-defense, Nance."

Nancy's voice dropped, her eyes staring into the distance as if seeing the memory replay in her mind. "I still... remember...the knife...going into her. The sound of it. I hear her screams in my head every day."

"You found the strength within to save us all. Well, except for..." Shelly's voice trailed off, her eyes welling up with tears.

Nancy's voice was choked with emotion. "I'm sorry."

"It's not your fault. It's not. I don't blame you," Shelly insisted.

"Brenda saved me. I panicked. I admit that. All I could do was run. I'm so sorry, Shelly," Nancy said, filled with guilt and sorrow.

"I know. I know," Shelly said, pulling Nancy into a tight embrace.

"You can sit this one out if you want. This is our chance to end this once and for all," Shelly presented with determination.

Nancy closed her eyes, guilt-ridden. Shelly's eyes stared out over Nancy's shoulder as they hugged, her mind focused on the task ahead.

CHAPTER 16: THE SPIRIT WORLD

The spirit world is as real and vivid as our own. This belief was what made Nancy nervous. The milieu was set, and that only sharpened the tenterhooks she was on. The living room of the cabin was dimly lit, the shifting light from numerous candles casting eerie penumbra. Modest summoning candles were delicately arranged on a round table, surrounding a torn, isolated picture of Angela Smazmoth, taken from the yearbook, placed in the center next to a clear crystal ball, a bowl of nuts, and a piece of bread. The mood was dark and deep, starkly contrasting the usual warmth of the room.

The women sat around the table, holding hands in a circle. Shelly squeezed Linda's hand, glancing at her with a determined look. She winked and nodded, signaling that it was time to begin.

"We summon thee, Angela Smazmoth. We call to thee. Are you here? Please give us a sign," Shelly intoned steadily.

There was no response. Everyone's eyes remained closed, the silence thick and oppressive.

Nothing.

Shelly's voice grew more insistent. "Angela Smazmoth, we demand your presence from the spirit world. You must come forth!"

Mary, her eyes still closed, quipped, "Demand? Maybe she's busy doing spirit things."

Ignoring the remark, Shelly continued, "Angela. Smazmoth. I know you can hear me! Come forth! Give us a sign! Commune with us and move among us."

Suddenly, Linda began to shake and speak in a ridiculous, theatrical manner. "I speak with the spirit of Smangela Azmoth!"

Shelly nudged her sharply. "I mean Angela Smazmoth! That is my name," Linda corrected herself, trying to sound more convincing.

Nancy sighed, now understanding the nature of the charade.

"Angela. We have brought you here today to ask if you would forgive Nancy for killing you," Shelly said slowly and deliberately.

Linda, now fully immersed in her role, exaggerated her spooky voice. "I forgive Nancy for killing me. It is not her fault. She did what she had to do."

Nancy's eyes remained closed, her mind swirling with memories. The room grew cold around her, an unsettling chill that seemed to seep into her very bones. She opened her eyes, but the vision that greeted her was unexpected and terrifying.

Nancy found herself in a dark, oppressive shack. The sounds of groaning, a heartbeat, distant screams, and a blender filled the air, creating a cacophony of madness. An apparitional Angela Smazmoth glided toward her, her blood-stained gown giving off a piercing glow. Nancy tried to close her eyes and escape the vision, but it was useless. Angela continued to advance, reaching out with spectral hands.

Back in the cabin, Linda opened her mouth to speak more, but Nancy interrupted in a raspy whisper, "I, Angela Smazmoth, am here!"

Shelly, Linda, Deborah, and Mary looked at Nancy in wonder as the crystal ball darkened from within and turned nightmare blue. Shelly, thinking Nancy was playing along, said, "Oh. Okay, Angela, restless spirit.

We understand your pain. We sense your anger on this earthly plane. We ask again for your forgiveness."

"Forgiveness?" Nancy rasped.

"Yes. Those who have caused you heartache and irreparable damage to Jimmy have been punished. Please, leave us in peace," Shelly pleaded.

A pregnant pause followed, the room overflowing with anticipation.

"You are forgiven. I will leave you in peace," Nancy replied.

The women seemed relieved, letting out breaths they hadn't realized they were holding.

"Thank you. Thank you very much. We really appreciate—" Shelly began, but Nancy cut her off.

"My son will come. He will find you. He will avenge me. You will know pain and suffering and blood!"

"Wait, what?" Shelly stammered.

Mary looked around, confused. "Is this not part of the show?"

Nancy turned her gaze to Mary. "You! Beauty is skin deep, but you hide an ugly soul."

Mary looked nervous. "Excuse me?"

Nancy's gaze shifted to Deborah. "Look at you! You care more about protests than people."

Deborah, taken aback, asked, "Nancy, what are you doing?"

Nancy turned to Linda. "You. Second fiddle. Too pathetic for words."

Linda's eyes welled up with tears. That cut deep.

Nancy's final gaze fell on Shelly. "You're all about peace and love, but you seethe with rage and jealousy."

Shelly was visibly freaked out. "You can leave us now, Angela."

"You'll be thrown from your high horse in no time," Nancy retorted.

"We thank you, but you can leave!" Shelly insisted.

Nancy's voice grew colder. "You're all the same. Holding on to guilt and begging for the forgiveness you don't deserve. My angel of death is coming. You will all pay."

In a desperate attempt to end the séance, Shelly blew out the candles and disrupted the setting. Nancy let out a raspy laugh, and Smash-Mouth's face flashed before her eyes for a moment. She screamed and snapped out of the trance, her eyes wide with terror.

"Did you see it? Did you see him? He was here!" Nancy cried.

Trying to make sense of it all, Mary asked, "What are you talking about?"

"Who did you see?" Shelly demanded.

The crystal ball was now clear again, and the bread offering was moldy. Nancy looked around, then broke away from the table and ran upstairs. Mary clicked on the lights, and the shaken women gathered around the table.

"What the hell was that?" Mary asked in a trembling shout.

"Yeah, seriously. She stepped on all of my lines," Linda added.

"What?" Mary asked, confused.

"Nothing. Linda's just being a drama queen. Right, drama queen?" Shelly retorted, trying to regain control of the situation.

"You've gone too far with this séance thing," Linda shot back.

"Me?!" Shelly replied, incredulous.

"You pushed her into it. She's obviously not doing as well as you think," Linda accused.

Trying to mediate, Deborah said, "Maybe this retreat was a bad idea. She needs a doctor."

Mary, almost muttering under her breath, said, "If she's nuts, I'm nuts. We're all nuts." Noticing the bowl of nuts on the table near her, she exclaimed, "Oh, nuts!" She laughed nervously, took a nut from the bowl, and ate it.

"I agree with Deb," Linda said firmly.

"Are you trying to grow a brain on me, Linda?" Shelly snapped.

Mary and Deborah exchanged incredulous glances.

"What? No. I just..." Linda stammered.

"You were horrible to Jimmy Smazmoth," Shelly accused.

"We all were. Everyone treated him like the freak he was," Linda admitted.

"Cool your jets, Linda," Shelly warned.

"Fine! But I hope you realize someday soon that your shit stinks just like everyone else's," Linda retorted before storming off upstairs.

Shelly stood speechless, Linda's words hanging.

"Great séance, Shel," Mary said sarcastically.

The cabin was filled with a heavy silence, each woman lost in her thoughts, grappling with the unsettling events that had just transpired. The bonds of friendship that had temporarily seemed so strong now felt fragile, strained by the continuing difficulties of coping with their shared past and now the ghost of Angela Smazmoth that they thought might still be lingering in their midst.

CHAPTER 17: THE WATCHER IN THE WOODS

The owl, for all his feathers, was a-cold. Thick with shadows, the moon cast an eerie glow over the landscape. The air was cool and damp, filled with the rustling of leaves and that shivering occasional call of that distant owl. Someone was watching through the windows, heavy breathing mingling with the sounds of the night. The creepy hillbilly, a flask in hand, peered through the glass, his eyes filled with a mix of curiosity and disdain.

"Goddamn hippies," he muttered under his breath, taking a swig. The sour smell of alcohol blended with the earthy scent of the forest as he stepped away from the window, heading off for a nearby trail.

The trail was narrow and winding, barely discernible in the dark. The hillbilly stumbled as he navigated the uneven ground, the alcohol in his system making him less steady on his feet. He mumbled, cursing the city folks who had invaded his territory.

Each step was accompanied by the crunch of leaves and twigs underfoot, sounds amplified in the stillness of the night.

As he walked, the hillbilly's thoughts wandered. He remembered the good old days when the forest was his alone before the cabins and tourists arrived. His life had been simple and uncomplicated by the outside world. Now, he felt like an intruder in his own home, pushed out by people who didn't understand the land the way he did.

After what felt like an eternity of walking, he stumbled upon an old shack hidden deep in the woods. It was a dilapidated structure, barely standing against the elements. The wooden planks were rotting, and the roof sagged ominously. Intrigued, he approached the shack, his interest piqued despite his initial reluctance.

He peered through a grimy window, straining to see inside. The interior was dimly lit, outlines creeping on the walls from a single, weak bulb hanging from the ceiling. The hillbilly could make out vague shapes and forms but nothing distinct. His curiosity getting the better of him, he decided to investigate further. He reached for the door handle, hesitating momentarily before pushing it open. The door creaked loudly on its rusty hinges, the sound weaving through the woods.

Stepping inside, the hillbilly was immediately hit by the musty smell of death and decay. He was familiar with this odor from hunting, but this was more oppressive than anything he had previously encountered. The air was congested and oppressive, making it hard to breathe.

A hideous figure stood silently in the corner of the shack, draped in a tattered football uniform. The sight was jarring, the uniform stained and worn, as if it had seen decades of decay.

"What in tarnation?" the hillbilly shouted. He took a tentative step closer to get a better look at the figure.

Before he could react, a sledgehammer cracked his skull from behind. He stumbled, trying to regain his balance, but a tall figure in black loomed over him, the door slamming shut with a resounding thud. Panic set in as he realized he was trapped.

The hillbilly was slammed down onto a cold, hard slab in the center of the shack. He struggled, his screams resonating in the confined space. "No! Please, oh God, no!" he cried, desperation clear in his voice. His pleas were met with silence, the only response being the methodical movements of the figure above him.

The hammer again descended with brutal force, striking his skull. He fell back, dazed, his vision blurring. His eyes crossed, the world around him spinning into a chaotic blur of pain and fear. The room seemed to tilt and sway, the dim light overhead decaying ominously.

A cleaver was raised, catching the dim light. The hillbilly looked up in horror. The cleaver came down with a sickening thud, then was raised again, streaked with blood. The disturbing rhythm continued, each swing bringing a new wave of agony.

He screamed, his voice raw and filled with terror. The sound of a blender turning on filled the air, the blades spinning with a menacing whirr. Severed fingers and bloody chunks of flesh were thrown into the blender, the repulsive mixture transforming into a sickening puree. The noise was deafening, drowning out his cries.

The concoction was poured into a barely washed glass, a straw sticking out from the top. From the dark corner, wicked hands reached out, eagerly grasping the glass. Sickening slurping sounds filled the shack, the figure in the tattered football uniform greedily consuming the macabre meal.

The hillbilly had heard that your whole life flashes before your eyes at the moment just before you die, but he doubted such old wives' tales could be true. Nonetheless, despite his skepticism, that's just what happened to hillbilly Robert Hickson.

In the sepulchral depths of Appalachia, Robert Hickson's existence unfurled like a sorrowful ballad. Born on a frostbitten January morning in 1922, Robert's early years were a symphony of chainsaws, the sonorous thud of falling timber, and the olfactory wash of fresh pine. His father, Thomas Hickson, was an austere man, chiseled by years of arduous labor and the inexorable pressure of providing for his kin in an unforgiving terrain.

Robert's mother, Daisy, was a personification of kindness and sacrifice. Her hands were marred from years of laundering clothes in the frigid creek and nurturing their parsimonious vegetable garden. Despite the unabated hardship, Daisy found time to read to Robert and his siblings by the sputtering light of an oil lamp, her dulcet tones weaving tales of distant realms and heroic sagas. These stories were ephemeral escapes for Robert, fleeting reprieves from the grinding reality of his quotidian life.

As a child, Robert was introverted and contemplative, traits that rendered him a convenient target for the local ruffians at the one-room schoolhouse he attended. His tattered attire and perpetually soiled hands marked him as an outlier, and children can be ruthlessly cruel. The jeers and taunts left indelible scars on Robert's psyche, compelling him to withdraw further into his solitude, finding solace in the embrace of the forest.

At thirteen, a calamity struck. His mother succumbed to pneumonia, and despite their fervent efforts, the local doctor's ministrations were futile. Her demise left a vacuum in the Hickson family, one that Thomas attempted to fill with even more obdurate toil and sterner discipline. The warmth and luminescence Daisy had bestowed upon their home were extinguished, casting Robert's world into deeper umbrage.

By sixteen, Robert had forsaken his education to labor alongside his father and elder brother, Sam. The labor was grueling, the recompense paltry, but it was their only means of subsistence. Sam, the more gregarious and charismatic sibling, enlisted in the army at eighteen, leaving Robert in solitary company with their increasingly embittered and reclusive father. The seclusion of their woodland abode mirrored the isolation festering within Robert's heart.

Years elapsed in monotonous drudgery. Robert's routine was a somber litany of pre-dawn risings, chopping wood, or hunting game, followed by evenings spent imbibing cheap whiskey by the fire, the forest's nocturnal harmonies his only companion.

In his early thirties, Robert's father passed away, felled by years of backbreaking labor and intemperate drinking. Robert interred him in an unmarked grave behind their cabin, the act imbued with a stoic finality. Alone, the solitude that had been a constant specter in Robert's life now enveloped him completely.

The forest was his retreat. He knew every arboreal path, every babbling brook, and every creature's trail. The woods offered refuge, a haven from the unceasing desolation that pervaded his existence. His days were spent wandering, foraging for sustenance, and occasionally finding employment as a handyman or hunter for the townsfolk who pitied him or required his expertise.

One particularly harsh winter, Robert's situation became dire. Game was scarce, and the cold was unyielding. He stumbled upon an abandoned house deep within the woods, which became his refuge against the biting winds and unrelenting hunger. He fortified it as best he could, using whatever detritus nature provided. As the days stretched into weeks, his thoughts turned increasingly bleak. The isolation, the unceasing struggle for survival, and the haunting memories coalesced into a pervasive and dejected ferity.

With the arrival of spring, the house began to feel like a semblance of home. However, the specters of his past remained unvanquished. He decided to leave the only place he had ever known. Tales of vast, unspoiled landscapes and new opportunities in the West beckoned him. The notion of a fresh start, far from those ghosts of his past, grew increasingly alluring. He gathered his meager possessions and embarked on an odyssey to find solace.

The journey was arduous, fraught with peril. Robert traversed rugged mountains, forded icy rivers, and endured capricious weather, relying on his wits and the survival skills honed in the Appalachians. Each step distanced him from the dark memories, yet the indelible scars they left remained a constant reminder of the life he sought to escape.

Eventually, Robert found himself amidst a sprawling, dense woodland far from his familiar haunts. Here, he hoped to find the peace and solitude that had always eluded him. He constructed a new abode, fortifying it against the elements, and resumed his life of quiet isolation.

Despite the tranquility of his new surroundings, memories of his mother and father and the life he had known in Appalachia were never far from his thoughts. The wounds inflicted by years of hardship and loss ran deep, and the solitude that defined his existence was an ever-present companion.

In a serene stillness, surrounded by the symphony of nature, Robert Hickson persevered in his solitary existence. The primal tasks of survival consumed his days, his nights haunted still by the very same specters of a past, an ever-looming reminder of the life he had left behind.

Now, as Robert's flame burned out, a victim of a war he had simply stumbled into, these Cimmerian memories left his body as he navigated the final crepuscular journey through the liminal space between life and death.

The hillbilly's vision faded, and the last thing he saw was the horrific sight of his own flesh being consumed.

The night outside remained silent, the petrifying tableau within the shack hidden from the world. The hillbilly's screams faded, swallowed by the oppressive silence of the forest. The moon continued to cast its eerie glow, indifferent to the horrors unfolding beneath its light.

CHAPTER 18: NANCY FROM

Everyone at Donner High had the story, bit by bit, from various people, and, as generally happens in such cases, each time, it was a different story. Nancy's story was not the story of Shelly. And though one might view one as a villain and one as a hero, each person is a hero in their own story and a villain in another's. Shelly's séance created only villains and only had perspectives driven by dread and augury.

Nancy retreated to her room, her heart pounding in her chest. The events of the evening had left her shaken, her nerves frayed. She closed the door behind her, leaning against it momentarily as she tried to collect herself. The room was dimly lit by the single lamp on the bedside table, casting long shadows on the walls. She moved to the edge of her bed, sinking onto the soft mattress.

Taking deep breaths, Nancy tried to calm herself. She felt the memories she had long tried to bury resurfacing with a vengeance. Her mind was a storm of thoughts and emotions, each more unsettling than the last. She could still hear Angela's voice and feel the cold grip of fear that had taken hold of her during the séance.

A sudden draft from the window caught her attention. The cool air gave her goosebumps, and she turned to close the window. As she did, something in the glass made her blood run cold. Smash-Mouth's deformed reflection appeared, and his grotesque features warped into a grin. She gasped, spinning around to face the room, her heart racing.

But there was no one there. The room was empty, silent except for the sound of her own ragged breathing. She looked back at the window, hoping it had been a trick of the light. But there he was again, Smash-Mouth, his face looming in the glass.

"Go away!" Nancy shouted. She backed away from the window, her eyes wide.

The reflection did not move, did not waver. It was as if he was truly there, just beyond the glass, watching her. Was this real? Was she losing her grip on reality? The line between memory and imagination had blurred, leaving her trapped in a nightmare from which she could not wake.

She remembered the first time she had encountered Angela's Smash-Mouth, and the terror that had gripped her then was nothing compared to the horror she felt now seeing this hallucinatory vision of Jimmy's real face. Back then, she had been fighting for her life, driven by adrenaline and the instinct to survive. Now, she was battling her own mind, the memories, and guilt gnawing at her sanity.

Nancy closed her eyes, trying to push the image away. But even with her eyes shut, she could still see him. She could hear his laughter, a haunting reverberation through her thoughts. The past bore down on her, an unfaltering force that threatened to crush her.

"Go away," she cried again, trembling. She hugged herself, trying to find some comfort within the room's emptiness. She remembered the night Angela had died, the feel of the knife in her hand, the sound of it piercing flesh. The horror of that moment had never left her, a permanent scar on her soul. She had killed to survive, but the guilt had never faded. It had festered inside her, a constant reminder of what she had done.

And now, it seemed, the past had returned to haunt her. Smash-Mouth, the debased embodiment of her guilt and fear, was here, lurking in the trenches of her mind.

She felt trapped, unable to escape the nightmare that had become her reality.

Nancy opened her eyes, forcing herself to look at the window again. The reflection was gone, but the fear remained. She moved to the window, closing it firmly and drawing the curtains shut. She turned back to the room, feeling a momentary sense of relief.

But it was fleeting. The shadows still loomed, and the memories still haunted her. She knew that closing the window would not keep the past at bay. Smash-Mouth, Angela, the horrors she had endured—they were all part of her, ingrained in her psyche.

Nancy sat back down on the bed, her body trembling. She pulled her knees to her chest, wrapping her arms around them. She needed to find a way to fight this, to reclaim her peace of mind. But how could she fight something that was part of her, something that lived in her memories?

"Go away," she roared one last time. She closed her eyes, trying to find some semblance of calm in the void.

She knew that the psychic battle was far from over, but she was determined to find a way to face it. She had survived before, and she would survive again. But the journey would be long, and she would need all the strength she could muster to see it through. She had no idea that this psychic war would not be the worst thing she had to worry about tonight. She did not yet know that Jimmy was very real and very close.

CHAPTER 19: THE FRACTURED SEAL

In the beginning, this war was but a whisper. Now, everyone was a soldier of their own. The atmosphere in the cabin was pullulating with tension as Deborah, Mary, and Shelly began to clean up the séance table. The candles were extinguished, the residue of their ritual scattered across the table. The picture of Angela Smazmoth was torn and crumpled, a silent corroboration of the chaos that had unfolded. Shelly moved mechanically, her mind clearly elsewhere.

"What's wrong, Shelly?" Mary asked, noticing her friend's withdrawn demeanor.

Shelly sighed, her eyes distant. "I should check on Linda. That was a buzzkill."

"Go ahead. We've got this under control," Mary reassured her.

Shelly nodded and headed upstairs. Deborah and Mary continued cleaning, but their movements were more subdued now. At least this task could occupy their troubled minds for the moment, so the longer it went on, the better.

"I've never seen Linda stand up to Shelly like that," Deborah whispered, glancing toward the stairs.

"I know. Usually, she's such a—" Mary began, but her words were cut off by a piercing scream from upstairs. It was Shelly.

Mary and Deborah's hearts leaped into their throats. They dropped everything and sprinted toward the source of the scream, fear gripping them.

They burst into Linda's room, their eyes widening in horror. Linda lay on the floor, covered in blood, wearing an old leather football helmet, eerily similar to the one Jimmy Smazmoth used to wear. The sight was nightmarish, the blood stark against her unblemished skin.

Already on edge, Nancy rose sharply from her bed at the sound of Shelly's scream. Her heart pounding, she reached into a drawer and pulled out a pair of scissors. She stepped into the hallway, her breath coming in quick, shallow gasps, and made her way toward Linda's room.

In Linda's room, Shelly, Mary, and Deborah stood frozen, reacting in horror to the scene. Nancy knelt down to check on Linda, her movements deliberate, her mind racing with fear and dread.

Suddenly, Linda's eyes fluttered open, and she smiled. "You all should see the looks on your faces," Linda joked.

Shelly started to laugh nervously, relief flooding through her. "What?! Linda!"

Nancy, however, just stared at Linda coldly. She had no fear or tears left, only a deep, burning anger. She rose, her eyes locked on a chuckling Shelly.

"Good to know you'd jump right into battle mode if any of us were in danger. You still got that killer instinct, it seems," Shelly said to Nancy, her tone light but with an undercurrent of something darker.

Nancy said nothing, stepping out into the hallway, unimpressed and simmering with silent rage.

"Jesus, Linda," Mary muttered, shaking her head as she followed Nancy.

Mary approached Nancy in the hallway. "Are you okay?"

Nancy let out a shaky breath, her eyes haunted. "I actually thought I was losing it. I really did. I've been seeing Jimmy Smazmoth all around since we got here. All this time, it was Linda."

Deborah stepped out of Linda's room, her expression a mix of anger and exhaustion. "I've had enough of this Smazmoth shit for one night."

From inside the room, Linda's voice carried a defensive tone. "Deb, it was just a joke."

Deborah shot back cold and hard, "Jokes are funny."

Deborah shut the door behind her with a decisive click. She glanced at Nancy and Mary, deep in conversation, their expressions tense and weary.

"I need some air," Deborah muttered, brushing past them and heading downstairs.

Inside Linda's room, Linda grinned at Shelly, a mischievous glint in her eyes. "Well, you thought it was funny."

Shelly shook her head, though a smile tugged at her lips. "You're a jerk."

They both laughed, the tension between them easing.

"I'm sorry I snapped at you before," Shelly added.

Linda shrugged, her grin widening. "Consider this payback. We're even."

As their laughter filled the room, the lingering fear and tension from the night's events began to dissipate.

But outside, in the hallway and beyond, the demons and the fallen angels of their past still loomed large, waiting for the right moment to resurface.

CHAPTER 20: ECHOES OF THE WAR

There are few things in life more pathetic than those who have been great and are not. Those who left behind their acme of greatness in high school rest even lower on the food chain. Nancy and Mary made their way down the cabin stairwell. Both women were desperate for a moment of respite.

"We haven't had a moment of relaxation since we got up here," Mary remarked.

"I didn't really expect to, but this is even worse than I thought it would be," Nancy replied, her mind still replaying the horrors of the evening.

They arrived downstairs, the familiar warmth of the kitchen offering a brief respite from their troubling thoughts. Mary and Nancy grabbed some snacks and beverages, leaning against the counter as they chatted, trying to find some normalcy amidst the chaos.

"What happened to you during the séance?" Mary asked, her eyes searching Nancy's for understanding.

Nancy took a deep breath, recalling the surreal experience. "I couldn't move. It felt like I was tied to my chair. I couldn't see any of you. I was in another place. I saw Angela. I heard her voice coming through me, but I had no control, and I couldn't make out the words."

Mary listened intently, trying to piece together the strange occurrences. "The stuff she said was pretty creepy, but I'm not sure what any of it meant. I don't know. You were the last to see her alive. It makes sense that she'd still have a connection to you to..." She rolled her eyes, imitating a possessed person, "...channel through you. How do you feel now?"

"A little better, actually. It's strange, but I get the feeling that she has forgiven me," Nancy said, a slight sense of relief washing over her. Yet, a nagging doubt lingered in the back of her mind, an unease she couldn't quite shake.

Nancy's expression grew more serious. "One thing, though. I also saw Jimmy. But I don't think it was his spirit."

Mary's face paled slightly, her unease growing. She didn't respond, her thoughts swirling with the implications of Nancy's words.

They carried their snacks and beverages into the billiards room, seeking distraction in the familiar game of pool. The room was cozy, and the polished wood of the pool table invited them to forget their troubles for a while. They racked up the balls, filling the room with a clicking and clacking.

Nancy took the first shot, focusing on the game, which offered a brief escape from the haunting memories. The balls scattered, their movement a temporary distraction from the night's events.

Mary watched Nancy, her thoughts still on the conversation they had just had. She was unnerved by the idea of Jimmy's presence, even if it wasn't his spirit. She tried to shake off the feeling, focusing on her turn as she lined up her shot.

"Do you really think it was Angela's spirit forgiving you?" Mary asked, breaking the silence.

Nancy nodded slowly. "I think so. I felt a sense of peace, but there is something else. It's like a warning, a sense that something is still wrong."

Mary took her shot, the clack of the balls punctuating her thoughts. "Do you think it has to do with Jimmy? I mean, he was always...different."

Nancy's eyes narrowed, her mind racing. "It's possible. But what if it's not Jimmy? What if it's something else, something we haven't even considered?"

Mary shivered, the thought sending chills to her extremities. "Let's just try to enjoy this moment. We need a break from all this."

They continued to play, the game's rhythm comforting. Each shot and movement was an attempt to reclaim some sense of normalcy. As they played, Nancy's mind kept drifting back to the vision of Jimmy. She couldn't shake the feeling that he wasn't a figment of her imagination. There was a gloam, a malevolence that she couldn't quite understand. It was as if the past was reaching out to them, refusing to let go.

Mary, sensing Nancy's distraction, tried to lighten the mood. "Remember when we used to play pool in high school? You always beat me."

Nancy smiled faintly, appreciating the effort. "Yeah, those were simpler times. I wish we could go back to that."

"But we can't," Mary said softly, her eyes reflecting the same sadness. "We can only move forward."

Nancy nodded, taking another shot. "Yeah, I guess you're right. We just have to figure out how to do that without losing our minds."

Mary spoke cautiously, "Sometimes I think about what people say about Vietnam."

Nancy looked at her, curiosity piqued. "What do you mean?"

Mary sighed, her gaze distant. "I mean, it's like there's this constant battle. Not just out there in the jungles, but in here too," she said, tapping her temple. "It's a war against memories, against the things we've done and seen."

Nancy nodded reluctantly. "We're fighting our own battles. I don't know if it's really comparable to war."

Mary pushed further. It was uncharacteristic of the Mary of 15 years prior to speak about anything other than boys or fashion, but perhaps she was altered in her own way that Nancy had not yet noticed. Maybe it was not just Nancy who had been changed forever. "It's like we're soldiers, each dealing with our own personal war. We came out of that nightmare changed, and now we're trying to find our way back to some kind of normal. It's like those stories you hear about soldiers coming home.

They may leave the battlefield, but the battlefield never really leaves them."

Nancy understood. "In a way, we have our own Vietnam. The horrors we faced, what we did to survive. Our battles. Some wounds are visible, but others are hidden deep inside."

Mary nodded. "And just like the soldiers, we're trying to find a way to cope, to heal. But it's not easy. The past creeps up, no matter how far you try to run."

Nancy sighed. "You're right. I guess all we can do is keep fighting. Not with weapons, but with hope. Maybe one day, we'll find peace."

The room fell silent again, each woman lost in her thoughts. And in that moment, they felt a little closer, still bound by their shared experiences, but now also the hope that they would someday find a way to heal.

They played in silence for a while. The game was a temporary escape, a moment of calm in the storm of their lives. The feeling of unease never entirely left Nancy. There was a constant reminder that their troubles were far from over. And as they played, the night outside grew darker, the shadows more profound, and the past ever closer, still waiting patiently for its moment to return.

CHAPTER 21: THE NIGHT'S CHILD

Under the cloak of darkness, secrets were whispered, and shadows danced. Deborah stepped out of the cabin, the cool night air starkly contrasting the oppressive atmosphere inside. She needed a moment to herself, away from the tension and the ghosts of the past that seemed to haunt every corner of the cabin. She walked down to an overlook deck, where she could clear her mind and breathe freely.

The deck offered a stunning view of the forest below. The trees swayed gently in the breeze, their leaves shaking out secrets into the night. Deborah took in the scenery, allowing the beauty of nature to soothe her frayed nerves. She reached into her pocket, pulled out a cigarette, and lit it with practiced ease. The first drag was deep and calming, the familiar burn, a comfort amid her turmoil.

Deborah started smoking when she was sixteen, drawn to the habit by the iconic image of James Dean, the epitome of cool rebellion. It was the 1950s, and James Dean was the poster boy for youthful defiance and misunderstood angst. His smoldering gaze and the ever-present cigarette between his lips made smoking seem like an essential accessory for anyone wanting to project an aura of effortless popularity.

She remembered watching *Rebel Without a Cause* for the first time, mesmerized by Dean's portrayal of Jim Stark. Every scene where he lit up, exhaling wisps of smoke, seemed to imbue him with an air of mystery and subversion that Deborah found irresistible. It wasn't just the act of smoking; it was the way he held the cigarette, the way he inhaled deeply as if drawing power from it, and the way he exhaled with a languid grace that suggested he was above it all. To Deborah, it symbolized freedom and resistance against societal expectations, a way to transcend the limitations of youth and sex.

In fact, it was on her sixteenth birthday that she snuck out to buy her first pack of cigarettes. She chose the same brand she had seen James Dean use in the movies, hoping to capture even a fraction of that enigmatic charm. The first drag made her cough, the acrid smoke burning her throat and lungs. But she persevered, practicing in front of the mirror until she

142

could mimic Dean's casual elegance. Each puff was a step closer to the image she wanted to project—an image of detachment and nonchalance.

Smoking quickly became part of her identity. It was more than a habit; it was a statement. She found a strange camaraderie with other like-minded rebels in the smoky haze of high school bathrooms and behind the gym. They were a small, tight-knit group, bound by their shared deliberate insubordination and a desire to emulate their screen idol. The tobacco scent intertwined with her memories of adolescence, stolen moments, and secure secrets.

Even as the years passed and the health risks of smoking became widely known, Deborah clung to her cigarettes. She had already committed ten years to the habit by the time the Surgeon General's warnings appeared. Those adjurations backfired and served as exhortations, giving her an even greater sense of being that rebel she longed to become. At first, she was without cause, but she quickly adopted the civil rights movement and the newly emerging era of feminist thought and action.

Throughout all of the changes, the cigarettes were there for her. They were a link to her past, a reminder of the girl who had once dreamed of shedding her femininity to emulate Dean. The cigarettes were a part of her, just as much as her memories of Nancy and the unspoken feelings that lingered between them.

As she smoked, Deborah's thoughts drifted to the events of the evening. The séance, Nancy's trance, Linda's prank—it all felt surreal, like a perverse nightmare from which she couldn't wake. She flicked her ash, watching the glowing embers fall and fade into the tenebrosity below. The cold began to seep into her bones, and she rubbed her arms for warmth, feeling a shiver run through her.

With a sigh, she decided it was time to head back into the cabin. She started the short walk back, her footsteps reverberating softly on the wooden deck. Just as she neared the door, a noise caught her attention. She stopped, her senses suddenly on high alert. The breeze rustled the leaves, but that was not what she heard. There was something else she could feel but not see.

Deborah strained to listen, her heart beginning to race. "Is someone—?" she began.

The answer came not in words but in a sudden, brutal force. A football, wrapped in barbed wire, struck her hard in the face. The pain was immediate and blinding, a sharp agony that sent her reeling. She fell to the ground, the tiny remains of her cigarette slipping from her fingers and extinguishing on the cold, damp earth.

Her mind spun in chaos, the world around her blurring as she struggled to comprehend what had happened. The salty taste of blood filled her mouth, and she could feel the rough scrape of the barbed wire tearing into her skin again and again. Panic surged through her, but she was too dazed to move, too overwhelmed by the sudden attack.

The night closed in around her, the peacefulness of the forest shattered by the unexpected act of violence. Deborah's vision began to fade, the edges of her field of view darkening as she lay there, vulnerable and alone. The last thing she heard was a gentle, rhythmic psithurism carrying her into unconsciousness.

CHAPTER 22: WHISPERS OF THE NIGHT

That gentle rustle of leaves in the wind sounded like secrets being shared, and Nancy had finally decided that she needed to speak with Deborah about what had happened during the séance. It was time to share her secrets. She hoped that maybe a heart-to-heart conversation outside could clear the air. The cabin felt stifling, filled with too many bad memories and heightened emotions. She pulled on a sweater and stepped out the front door, seeking solace in the cool night air.

The treetops swayed gently in the wind, creating a soothing consonance. Nancy closed her eyes, allowing the sounds to wash over her, trying to accept this moment of peace amidst the chaos of the evening.

A noise broke her reverie. Her eyes snapped open, and she looked around, her senses on high alert. She glanced over to the overlook deck and froze. Deborah lay face down, blood pooling around her head.

Annoyance flared within Nancy, quickly replacing her initial concern. "Really, Deborah? You, too? Was this the plan all along? Let's scare Nancy to death?" she muttered angrily.

Deborah's body remained motionless, the preternatural stillness surrounding her. Nancy, convinced it was another prank, rolled her eyes. "I hope you're having fun laying here in the cold. I'm going to bed," she said, her irritation evident.

Without another glance, Nancy turned and went back inside the cabin, narrowly missing the sinister figures watching from the shadows. AJ and Smash-Mouth stood in the near distance, their shapes shrouded by the murk. As Nancy retreated indoors, they moved silently, dragging Deborah's lifeless body away into the depths of the woods.

Back inside, Nancy headed for the stairs, her thoughts consumed by irritation and exhaustion. As she reached the foot of the stairs, Mary and Shelly descended.

"I don't know what kind of far-out therapy you have planned for the weekend—" Nancy spit, laced with sarcasm and anger.

"Nancy—" Shelly interjected, trying to calm her friend.

"But the pranks have got to stop, okay? I'm done," Nancy continued, her frustration boiling over.

Shelly raised her hands in a placating gesture. "Nancy, relax. I talked to Linda. She won't do it again."

"Yeah? Good. Now go tell Deborah the same," Nancy shot back, her anger unabated.

Mary and Shelly exchanged a worried glance. They could see the strain in Nancy's eyes, the toll the night's events had taken on her. Shelly stepped forward. "Nancy, we need to talk."

Nancy shook her head, her mind too clouded by vexation to listen. "I'm done talking. I'm going to bed," she said, brushing past them and heading up the stairs.

As Nancy disappeared, Mary turned to Shelly and added, barely above a hush, "Do you think she saw Deborah?"

Shelly's expression was grim. "I don't know. But we need to find out where Deborah is. Now."

The two women exchanged a silent agreement and hurried toward the door.

Nancy's ire simmered as she climbed the stairs, each step alleviating a tiny fraction of her frustration.

She couldn't shake the feeling of being on edge, the pranks and scares grating on her already frazzled nerves. Reaching her room, she closed the door with a resolute thud, trying to shut out the bother of the night.

She sank onto the bed, her mind racing. Deborah's lifeless form on the deck had seemed so real, yet Nancy had convinced herself it was another cruel joke. As she lay back, staring at the ceiling, doubt began to creep in. What if it wasn't a prank? What if Deborah truly needed help?

Nancy sighed, feeling a pang of guilt. She knew she had to talk to the others, to clear the air and ensure they were all on the same page. The events of the night couldn't be dismissed so easily. She sat up, rubbing her temples, trying to dispel the headache forming from her tangled thoughts.

Her room felt colder than before, the iniquity pressing in from all sides. Nancy hugged herself, the gesture providing little comfort against the chill in her heart.

She remembered the strength in Deborah's eyes during their earlier conversation, the way she had spoken with such determination. That image clashed with the one of Deborah lying in a pool of blood, lifeless and alone. The contrast gnawed at Nancy, refusing to be ignored.

Suddenly, a soft knock at the door startled her. She froze, her heart racing. "Nancy, it's Mary. Come down when you can, please," came the muffled voice from the hallway.

Outside, the night continued its indifferent vigil, the trees hissing secrets to the zephyrs. Unbeknownst to the women inside the cabin, the true terror was only beginning in ways they could not yet comprehend.

CHAPTER 23: THE DISENCHANTED FOREST

There was something otherworldly about the collective organism of the forest, as if it once breathed and now held its breath in anticipation. AJ and Smash-Mouth traversed silently, the dim nocturnal glow casting their distorted shades on the ground. Perhaps this reflection of shadowiness from their bodies was a true reflection of their souls. The forest, alive now with the sounds of nocturnal creatures, disregarded their malignance as the two figures moved with a purpose that belied the serenity of their surroundings. They dragged Deborah's bloodied, lifeless body through the underbrush unyieldingly.

AJ's mind was a turbulent sea of thoughts as he toiled. He had once been an ordinary man, but years of rancor had mangled his psyche. The image of Deborah lying helplessly on the deck, struck down by their barbed-wire-wrapped football, replayed in his mind. He felt no remorse, only a grim satisfaction.

"She deserved it," AJ thought, his grip tightening on Deborah's arms. "They all do. They thought they could forget about us and move on. Well, they are about to learn a harsh lesson."

Smash-Mouth, moving beside him, remained a monstrous figure, a loathsome parody of the man he once was. His deformed features were hidden in the shadows, but his visage was unmistakable for anyone unfortunate enough to catch even a glimpse. A primal rage, an insatiable hunger for revenge and sustenance drove him. The taste of blood and flesh was a reminder of the power he held, the control he had over those who had once mocked and tormented him.

As they dragged Deborah's body deeper into the woods, the trees swallowed them. The path to the shack was well-worn, evidencing the many nights they had spent plotting and carrying out their revolting deeds. The silence of nature grew more oppressive as they neared their destination.

AJ glanced over at Smash-Mouth, who was staring straight ahead, his eyes gleaming with intensity. "We're almost there," AJ said, his voice low and steady. "Just a little further."

Smash-Mouth grunted in response, his breath visible in the cold night air. He was focused, his mind singularly attuned to the task at hand. Deborah was just another in a long line of victims. Her fate was sealed the moment she crossed their path.

The shack loomed ahead. For many, it was a symbol of terror, but for AJ and Smash-Mouth, this was their sacrarium, their fortress of vengeance. The door creaked open, and they dragged Deborah inside, her body leaving a trail of blood on the wooden floor.

AJ flipped on the single, flickering bulb, dimly lighting the shack's interior. AJ and Smash-Mouth worked in grim silence, their actions choreographed by years of practice.

AJ hoisted Deborah onto the cold, hard slab in the center of the room. Her body lay motionless. AJ stepped back, his eyes never leaving Deborah as Smash-Mouth approached with a hammer in hand.

"Make it quick," AJ said, his voice devoid of emotion. "We have work to do."

Smash-Mouth raised the hammer, the dim light glinting off its worn surface. With a swift, brutal motion, he brought it down on Deborah's skull. The sickening thud rang through the shack, followed by a second, then a third. Her body twitched with each impact, a reflex not indicative of her vitality.

AJ watched with a detached interest, his mind already moving to the next step. "Get the cleaver," he instructed, moving to prepare the blender, that barbaric relic, its blades stained with reminders of previous meals.

Smash-Mouth obeyed, retrieving the cleaver from a nearby table. He approached Deborah's body, his movements precise. He put great pride into his work and wanted AJ to recognize the effort, even if he didn't acknowledge it. The first cut was clean, severing Deborah's hand at the wrist. Blood spurted from the wound, pooling on the slab and dripping onto the floor.

AJ activated the blender, the blades whirring to life with a menacing hum. He took the severed hand from Smash-Mouth and tossed it into the blender without hesitation. The machine roared as it pulverized the flesh and bone, reducing it to a gruesome puree.

Smash-Mouth continued his work, dismembering Deborah's body with a disturbing efficiency. Each limb was removed and handed to AJ, who fed them to the blender one by one. The air was filled with the sounds of grinding metal and the sickening squelch of flesh being torn apart.

As they worked, AJ's thoughts drifted to the past. He remembered the days when they had been normal men, part of a community that had turned its back on them. The sense of betrayal had festered, transforming into this burning desire for revenge. Now, they were monsters, but they were powerful. And power, AJ had come to realize, was the only thing that mattered.

"Almost done," AJ muttered, wiping sweat from his brow. The blender was nearly full, an iniquitous mixture of blood and flesh. He poured the puree into a barely washed glass, a straw sticking out from the top.

Smash-Mouth reached out, his beastly hands trembling with anticipation. He grasped the glass, brought it to his lips, and drank deeply. The sickening slurping sounds filled the shack, an aural product of their sadistic bond.

AJ watched him, his own hunger sated by the knowledge that they had struck another blow against those who had wronged them. Deborah's death was just one more step in their campaign of vengeance, one more reminder that they would not be forgotten.

As Smash-Mouth finished his meal, AJ turned his attention back to the slab. What was left of Deborah's body lay there, a grisly tableau of their night's work. He still felt no remorse, only that same grim satisfaction. They had taken what they needed and, in doing so, had reclaimed a measure of the power stolen from them.

"We'll bury the rest in the morning," AJ said, his voice calm and controlled. "For now, let's clean up and get some rest. There's still much to do."

Smash-Mouth nodded, his repellent features softening slightly as the hunger ebbed. Together, they set about cleaning the shack, erasing the evidence of their abominable act. The night outside remained silent, the forest still indifferent to the horrors that had unfolded within.

As they worked, AJ's mind continued to churn. The satisfaction of their revenge was fleeting, but it was enough to sustain him for now. They had sent a message, one that would not be easily forgotten. And as long as they had each other, they would continue their dark work, ensuring that their names would be remembered in association with fear and infamy.

The shack and the stone altar within stood proudly as symbols of their resolve. Inside its walls, they held unassailable power. Even in that glory, AJ and Smash-Mouth knew that their campaign of vengeance was far from over.

CHAPTER 24: THE INVESTIGATION FOR DEBORAH

It was the kind of evening that sent shivers down the spine of even the most seasoned schizoaffective. Nancy could still hear the beleaguered ringing of Angela's dying voice. She could still feel the biting grip of fear. Even with the pranks and the betrayals, she knew she still had to speak with Deborah about what had happened during the séance to find clarity amidst the chaos. Resolutely, she pulled on a sweater, stepped out of her room, and headed downstairs.

Mary and Shelly were in the living room, clearly disquieted by how the night had gone. Though Shelly had mocked Nancy's reaction to Deborah's joke, she regretted it. Seeing Nancy, they approached hurriedly, hoping to address the confusion with Deborah.

"Nancy, come out with us," Mary said firmly.

Nancy hesitated. She didn't want to be alone with her thoughts, but the idea of more pranks made her queasy. "Okay, fine, but no more pranks," she replied, her tone wary.

The three women stepped outside into the chilly night, the dendriforms susurrating around them. As they walked toward the overlook deck, the night's lull was broken only by the soft crunch of their footsteps on the gravel path. Nancy's thoughts kept circling back to the séance, the voice of Angela, and the apparition of Jimmy.

Shelly's mind was racing, too. She felt a twinge of guilt about the séance. Had she pushed Nancy too far? She wanted to believe that everything happening was merely stress-induced paranoia, but the blood on the deck told a different story. She hoped desperately that Deborah was playing some kind of sick joke, but deep down, she feared the worst.

They arrived at the overlook deck, where the leavings of the night's horror lay starkly visible. Blood stained the wooden planks, and dragging marks led away into the dirt. Trawled footprints marred the ground, telling a story of violence and struggle.

"Deb? Deb, are you there?" Shelly called out, the desperate inquiry booming into the dim. There was no response, only the continuing rustle of the wind through the trees.

From the balcony above, Linda peered down, her face a mask of curiosity and very mild anxiety. "Hey, what's happening?" she called out.

"We can't find Deb," Shelly replied.

Linda shrugged nonchalantly. "Oh. She's probably off reading somewhere," she said, stepping back inside without another word.

Shelly turned to Nancy, her eyes narrowing with suspicion. "You said you saw her playing dead?"

Nancy met Shelly's gaze, her expression a mix of irritation and defensiveness. "She was right here. I figured it was another prank."

Shelly's eyes never left Nancy's face, her suspicion palpable. "What's on your mind, Shelly? Do you think I did something? Do you think I killed Deborah?" Nancy demanded incredulously.

"The furthest thing from my mind until you said it," Shelly replied coolly.

Nancy's eyes widened, her anger flaring. "Really?"

Shelly's tone was measured, her words deliberate and earnest, lacking her usual subtextual bite. "Angela used you as a conduit. What if some part of her remains?"

Nancy took a step closer. "May I remind you the séance was your idea, Shelly? I'm still me. Angela's long gone."

Mary stepped between them, "Look, now you two need to cool your jets. We need to find Deborah. Nancy, come with me."

Mary led the way inside the cabin, grabbing a couple of flashlights and a knife from a drawer in the foyer. She handed one of the flashlights to Nancy, her eyes severe. "Let's go, Nance."

Nancy felt a wave of gratitude for Mary's steady support. Despite the growing fear gnawing at her, she took comfort in having Mary by her side. They stepped back outside, the night air biting at their skin. But it didn't matter if they were cold now. They had a mission. The forest loomed around them, dark and foreboding. They followed the trail of blood and the dragging marks, their footsteps cautious and their eyes attentively scanning the woods.

Nancy tried to stay focused and alert as they walked. She couldn't shake the feeling that something terrible had happened, something far beyond the pranks and scares of the evening. The thought of Deborah lying hurt—or worse—somewhere deep in the woods filled her with dread. She tried to keep her mind centered, but the tortured image of Jimmy's face kept pushing back into her consciousness.

Mary, sensing Nancy's turmoil, tried to offer reassurance. "We'll find her, Nancy. We just have to stay the course."

Nancy nodded, gripping the flashlight tightly. "I hope you're right."

Mary couldn't help but replay the events of the evening in her mind. What if Shelly was right, and some part of Angela still lingered in Nancy? What if their tampering with the spirit world had real and permanent consequences? For the time being, though, she pushed the thoughts aside, focusing first on finding Deborah.

CHAPTER 25: THE HEARTS OF TWO LONELY HUNTERS

Even in high school, there were two extremes in this group, and they were always meeting together like a crushed horseshoe. Mary and Nancy, the two heels of that horseshoe, walked along the narrow trail, their flashlights cutting through the oppressive pitch. Every crunch of leaves and snap of a twig was amplified in the stillness. The tension grew, both women grappling with their fears and anxieties. Mary broke the silence, hoping to ease the situation a little bit.

"This weekend is just getting crazier, huh?" Mary said with nervous laughter.

Nancy sighed, her grip tightening on the flashlight. "This might be the worst day ever."

Mary let out a truncated laugh. She wasn't sure what Nancy was going for.

Nancy continued, "And I lived through a fight with a mass murderer."

Mary glanced at her, a wry smile tugging at her lips. She realized Nancy was trying to make some light of the situation. "A mass murderer who possessed you...and called me ugly?"

Nancy was intrigued. She couldn't really remember the specifics of the possession. Only the feelings and the images stuck with her. "Did she really say that? I hope she also said something mean to Shelly."

Mary's smile widened a bit. "She did!" Mary's laughter was genuine this time, though it quickly faded. "Look, Shelly means well. She's got the whole New Age, flower and Earth power thing going on."

Nancy's mood darkened. "I probably shouldn't have come here."

Mary went silent. She knew Nancy was struggling with more than just the events of the weekend.

"I'm sorry," Nancy said softly. "I am really glad to see you all. I do miss the good times."

Mary's heart ached for her friend. "So when we get back home, what happens then?"

Nancy's reply was firm, but there was a hint of uncertainty. "We put the past behind us and move on."

As they continued walking, Mary kicked something hard on the path. She stopped and looked down, her flashlight revealing a cigarette case lying in the dirt. It was Deborah's.

"That's not good," Mary murmured, her heart sinking.

The sound of a blender buzzing nearby broke the silence. It was crude, the noise indicating it was on its last legs. Mary and Nancy exchanged a horrified glance before following the sound, their fear growing with each step.

As they moved closer to the source of the unsettling sound, Nancy's thoughts drifted to the most recent summer and the moon landing. It symbolized human achievement, a testament to what was possible when people dared to dream. But it had also been the Summer of the Manson Family murders, a brutal reminder of the depravity lurking beneath the surface of society. The juxtaposition of those events had left a deep impression on her, a constant reminder that hope and horror were often intertwined. Like most everyone, she unfairly viewed cherry-picked world events as metaphors for her struggles. As she listened to the whir of the blender, she felt that dichotomy tugging at her soul.

Every step felt heavier, laden with their shared history and the unspoken fears that lingered between them. The sound of the blender grew louder, more menacing, as they approached, each pulse a grim portent of the hours ahead. They moved forward, driven by a mix of trepidation and a desperate need for answers, their hearts pounding in unison with the dogged beat of the night.

Mary's breath hitched as she thought of her brother, who she still thought of as a little kid reading *Man-Spider* comics, drafted and sent to Vietnam, a conflict that had scarred their family and left her with a deep-seated fear of loss. The senseless violence on the television and the constant dread of receiving the worst possible news had cast a long shadow over her life. That fear resurfaced now, with each rustle in the underbrush a potential threat. The realization of how fragile their safety truly was weighed heavily on Mary now.

As they neared the source of the sound, the memories blended with the present terror. Mary's flashlight caught a glimpse of movement ahead, and she froze, her heart hammering in her chest. Nancy's white knuckles wrapped tighter around her flashlight, her pulse quickening. They were on the brink of something terrible, and the burdens of the past threatened to crush their resolve.

At that moment, amidst the blender's roar and the woods' otherwise oppressive silence, Mary and Nancy stood united, their fears and memories uniting. They faced the turpitude together. The night was filled with horrors yet to be uncovered, but they moved forward with a determination borne of years of struggle and survival. The past had shaped them, but it would not define their fate.

CHAPTER 26: THE CALL OF SMASH-MOUTH

The most merciful thing in the world is the inability of the human mind to correlate all its contents. It allowed Nancy and Mary to proceed despite the apparent danger.

They stopped at a small clearing, the ground disturbed by the signs of a struggle. Blood stained the earth, and light dragging marks continued into the trees. Mary shone her flashlight around, her eyes narrowing as she tried to make sense of the scene.

"She was definitely dragged this way," Mary said steadily despite the fear in her eyes.

Nancy swallowed hard, her throat dry. "We have to keep going."

They followed the trail, their flashlights cutting through the vacant black. The air grew colder, the sense of dread more palpable with each step. The spin of the blender had subsided, and there was no longer any auditory map to their destination.

Suddenly, they heard a noise—a low, guttural growl that sent chills down their spines. They stopped, their breaths coming in quick, shallow gasps. Mary held the knife tightly and pointed the blade outward, ready to attack.

"Did you hear that?" Nancy mumbled.

Mary nodded. "Stay close to me."

They moved forward again cautiously, the growl growing louder as they approached. Their flashlights revealed a narrow path leading to a dilapidated shack.

"This must be it," Mary said with determination. "Stay behind me."

The path around Nancy and Mary seemed to grow darker as they approached, each movement condensing their rising fear. The towering trees loomed over them. Every sound was magnified—the rustling leaves, the distant call of an owl, and their own footsteps crunching on the duff.

Nancy couldn't shake the image of Deborah lying still and bloodied on the deck. She hoped against hope that Deborah was somehow alive, that this was all a horrible mistake. Her heart pounded in her chest, the fear and adrenaline making her feel lightheaded. She glanced at Mary, who walked beside her with a grim determination.

Mary's thoughts were equally chaotic. She had always prided herself on her strength and ability to remain calm under pressure, but this situation tested her limits. She kept thinking of the séance and the upsetting feeling of Angela's presence. It was as if the savagery from that night had followed them, consuming their reality.

They approached the shack, their footsteps slow and deliberate. The structure stood ominously in the clearing, its wooden planks rotting and roof sagging. The door creaked slightly with a push, revealing a dimly lit interior. The smell of decay and old blood rushed out. They peeked in through the slight opening.

Nancy gasped, her flashlight sweeping over the shocking scene. The sight of Deborah's bloodied body on the slab sent a wave of nausea through her. She fought to keep her composure, focusing on the task at hand. The stark reality of Deborah's lifeless form was almost too much to bear, the image burning itself into her mind.

Mary's voice was steady, but her eyes betrayed her fear. She felt a cold dread settling in her stomach. "We need to get out of here," Mary whispered forcefully. The words felt heavy and desperate in the quiet of the shack.

Nancy nodded, her mind still reeling from the horrors they had just witnessed. She couldn't stop thinking about the look on Deborah's face, the way her body lay so unnaturally still. "What about Deborah?" she asked.

Mary's eyes were filled with sorrow. She hated leaving Deborah behind, but their own survival had to come first. Mary also knew in her heart that Deborah was dead, but she would not fully admit this to herself and certainly not to Nancy. "We'll come back for her," she said regretfully.

Nancy's heart made its presence known in her chest, gastric acid rising into her esophagus as she watched. She fought to keep her composure through the revulsion. "We have to go. We have to go right now," she mouthed silently to Mary.

They both caught a glimpse of movement in the dark corner of the shack. Mary's eyes went wide with horror as she watched AJ hand a glass of the grisly puree to Smash-Mouth, who guzzled it down with sickening slurps and belches. She backed away, her stomach churning.

Suddenly, the shack door, which had just been cracked enough to allow observation, burst open all the way. Mary was pinned behind it, her flashlight clattering to the ground. Nancy moved out of the way, directly into AJ's line of sight. He grinned wickedly, grabbing her and pulling her inside the shack.

"Let her go!" Mary shouted, squeezing out from behind the door. Smash-Mouth raced out of the dark corner toward Mary, his arms outstretched, his face and jaw mangled and deformed in ways she could not have imagined. He was more horrific than his name had foretold.

Mary slammed the door into Smash-Mouth and took off through the woods, her heart pounding with fear and adrenaline. She ran as fast as she could, the branches whipping at her face and arms. Behind her, Smash-Mouth burst through the shack door, his football training kicking in as he pursued her with terrifying speed.

CHAPTER 27: THE PURSUERS

Smash-Mouth did not intend to explain how he came to be a hunter of men. The violence put upon him would become the violence he put upon others. There was no consideration, no other motivation, and certainly no hesitation.

Mary's lungs burned as she sprinted through the woods. She glanced back, seeing Smash-Mouth closing in on her. Desperation fueled her speed as she darted behind trees, trying to lose him in the density.

Smash-Mouth stopped, focusing on the footprints on the ground. He realized Mary was not ahead of him but somewhere around him. He listened intently, his senses sharp.

He heard her running footsteps heading in a specific direction. With a calculated pivot, he turned just in time to see Mary intentionally barreling toward him. This took him by surprise. No one had ever run at him since his transformation into this creature. Mary collided with him, knocking him to the ground.

Mary's mind was a blur of fear and determination. She stabbed at Smash-Mouth, the knife piercing his hand as he blocked her attack. He groaned in pain, the feral roar raising the hair on her neck.

She didn't wait to see the extent of the damage. Rising quickly, she took off running again. She could hear Smash-Mouth behind her, his pursuit unstoppable.

Mary's energy was spent, but she pushed herself to keep going, her thoughts filled with images of her friends, the séance, and the horrors she had witnessed. She couldn't let Smash-Mouth catch her. She had to survive, not just for herself but for Nancy.

Her legs went numb with pins and needles, and her lungs felt on fire, but she kept running, driven by sheer willpower. The sound of Smash-Mouth's footsteps grew fainter, but she knew he was still out there, hunting her.

Mary's mind raced, trying to come up with a plan. She needed to find a way to get back to the cabin and warn the others. She needed to figure out how to stop this nightmare once and for all.

As she ran, she thought of Nancy and the strength she had shown. If Nancy could survive a fight with a mass murderer and confront the ghosts of her past, then Mary could find a way to protect her friends and put an end to this.

How had things gone so wrong? What had they unleashed? She couldn't shake the image of Smash-Mouth's grotesque grin or the sound of his footsteps chasing her.

The trail ahead seemed endless, and her running slowed to a forced march at the demand of her corporeal limitations. Although she slowed, Mary's stubborn determination was unwavering. She knew the fight wasn't over, but she was ready to face whatever horrors lay ahead. She would survive, and she would ensure that her friends did, too.

Mary's muscles now screamed in protest and her ankles bent as she forced her legs to continue moving, the pain a constant reminder of her fragility in the face of such overwhelming danger. Each step was a Herculean effort, the ground beneath her seeming to conspire against her flight with roots and rocks that threatened to trip her up at every turn.

The television images of fire hoses, police dogs, and brave souls standing firm against an unjust system flashed before her eyes. Those pictures had modeled resilience and courage for her, qualities she now clung to as she fought to stay ahead of the unremitting predator somewhere behind her.

The forest canopy above filtered the moonlight into a ghostly glow, casting long, shifting shadows that played tricks on her vision. Every crackle and crunch of the thicket sent jolts of adrenaline coursing through her veins. The oppressive dark seemed almost sentient as if the woods themselves were conspiring to hide her pursuer and expose her every move.

She could hear Smash-Mouth's distant roars of frustration, but a surge of hope filled her as she finally broke through the tree line and saw the cabin in the distance. The sight of it gave her a renewed burst of energy, but she knew she had to be smart. She had to find a way to outwit Smash-Mouth and turn the tables in their favor.

Her mind was a whirlwind of strategies and desperate hopes. The cabin was a beacon of safety in the otherwise treacherous woods but also potentially a trap if she didn't approach it carefully. She had to warn the others without leading Smash-Mouth directly to them. The weight of this responsibility pressed heavily on her, but it also fueled her determination.

CHAPTER 28: THE TRIAL

Someone must have slandered Nancy, for this evening, without having done anything truly wrong, she was captured. The shack's interior was a perverted tableau of horrors. In the center of the room, Nancy struggled against her bindings, her wrists and ankles held tightly to a chair. The ropes cut into her skin, and she could feel the panic rising in her chest. She glanced around, her eyes landing on the figure of her captor.

"AJ?" she gasped, trembling with a mix of recognition and disbelief.

AJ, standing before her with a nefarious grin, nodded slowly. "You do remember," he said, his tone laced with dark amusement.

Nancy's gaze shifted to the fetid scene around her. There were several shakes made from the residuum of Deborah, her bloody clothes discarded carelessly on the ground nearby. The sight made Nancy's stomach churn, bile rising in her throat. The reality of the situation hit her like a freight train—Deborah was dead, and she would be next.

AJ picked up one of the bloody shakes, his expression one of corrupt satisfaction. "What were the odds?" he mused, more to himself than to Nancy.

Nancy's eyes teared as she pleaded, "AJ, please."

He ignored her, continuing his monologue. "We come out here for a little relaxation. Just some time to help my friend cope with the loss of his mother," he said, gesturing vaguely toward the unlit corners where Smash-Mouth had previously lurked. The mere mention of Smash-Mouth brought a wave of memories that repulsed her even further.

Nancy's voice cracked with desperation. "Please let me go. You can stop this."

AJ disregarded Nancy's pleas. His smile widened as he continued, a chilling sight in the dim light. "And we find you and a house full of future meals invading our space. How are you, Nancy? You look well."

She glanced again at Deborah's mutilated corpse. The sight was too much to bear, her friend's lifeless body an exigent reminder of the danger she was in. She could no longer contain her fear. "Look, we'll leave town. We won't tell anyone about—" She could not finish the sentence before AJ retook the authority to speak.

"Let you go? I can't let you go." AJ shook his head slowly.

He approached her with one of the bloody shakes in hand. The unimaginably vile concoction sloshed around in the cup. Nancy slowly realized his intentions. She fought harder against her bindings, her wrists raw and bleeding. The ropes tightened with every pull, cutting deeper into her flesh, but she continued to struggle.

"Not on an empty stomach," AJ said, his voice dripping with malevolence.

Nancy's eyes widened. "No," she yelped, shaking her head. She searched every outcome in her thoughts of escape, but every option seemed futile.

AJ tilted his head, his grin widening. "How well do you really know your friends?" he asked, holding up the glass.

Nancy's voice rose in panic. "No!"

AJ moved closer and placed his grip on her head like a vice. "How well do you really know, Deborah?" he taunted, pressing the bloody shake to her lips.

Nancy clamped her mouth shut, turning her face away to avoid the abhorrent blend. The smell was overwhelming, a mix of iron and decay that made her gag. "No!"

AJ's grip tightened, forcing her head back. "How well do you really know anyone!" he remonstrated.

He poured the bloody, chunky puree onto her lips, the foul mixture spilling down her chin. Nancy shook her face vigorously, desperately trying to avoid ingesting any of the splatter. The taste and smell were overwhelming, and she gagged, fighting back the urge to vomit. Her skin crawled with the sensation of the lumpy fluid coating her lips and chin.

"Eat it! Eat it, Nancy! There are hungry people all over the world! Don't let this perfectly good meal go to waste!" AJ yelled, his voice maniacal. His eyes gleamed with a sadistic pleasure, feeding off her fear and disgust.

Tears streamed down Nancy's face as she struggled, her body trembling. She was flooded with memories of her friends, their shared happy moments, and the horrific turn their reunion had taken. She couldn't let it end like this.

AJ's laughter rose in a sonic boom, shaking the room like a demonic chorus. Now, in the depths of her despair, Nancy had to find a way out. She had to survive this nightmare. The image of the friends she had fought so hard to protect 15 years prior flashed before her eyes. She had given up on Brenda. She couldn't give up now, not like this.

CHAPTER 29: THE CABIN AT THE END OF THE TRAIL

Far from the bustling towns and cities, Shelly's solitary cabin stood as a beacon of peace and isolation, however broken that sentiment. Out of breath and out of strength, Mary finally arrived at that false refuge and rushed inside, slamming the front door behind her and locking it with trembling hands. She hurried to the windows, pulling the curtains closed with quick, jerky movements. The house was eerily quiet; the only sound was the faint running of water upstairs.

"Shelly!" Mary called out.

Shelly appeared at the top of the stairs, worriment on her face as she took in Mary's dirty, disheveled appearance. "Mary, what happened? Where's Nancy?"

Mary's eyes were wide with fear. "We're in trouble. Jimmy Smazmoth is here. I couldn't believe it at first. They got Deborah."

Shelly's face went pale. "Deborah? Oh no."

Mary's urgency was palpable. "We need to lock the doors and windows. Everything."

Shelly shook her head, trying to process the information. "What? Wait a minute. What about Nancy? Where is she? Who's they?"

"AJ's got her," Mary replied.

"AJ? From high school, AJ?" Shelly asked, incredulous.

Mary nodded, her fear morphing into a cold, hard determination. "AJ and Jimmy. They're up here. I don't know how or why, but they're up here. The shack we saw!"

Shelly's eyes widened in shock. "Oh, my god."

"Jimmy just tried to kill me. I had to run. I had to," Mary said, bursting into tears.

Shelly nodded. "It's okay. We need to secure everything here, and then we can figure out what to do."

The two women sprang into action, checking around the house frantically, locking and closing windows. They focused on one thing—survival.

But they were not alone. Terror had arrived. From Smash-Mouth's point of view, just outside the sliding glass door, the house was a hive of activity. He watched Mary and Shelly move from window to window and door to door, securing the nest. His eyes gleamed with a predatory hunger, his breaths heavy with anticipation.

Despite his desire to pounce, Smash-Mouth held patiently outside that sliding door, his breath fogging the cool glass. His mind sinuated about with anger, pain, and dark satisfaction. As he watched Mary and Shelly moving frantically inside the cabin, memories of his past flickered through his mind.

In an endless loop like a rampaging stag reel, he remembered the taunts, the jeers, and the beatings he had endured at the hands of the football team. Each cruel word and punch had carved deep scars into his psyche and his body, turning his heart into a cold, hardened stone. The name "Smash-Mouth" had been given to him as a joke, a cruel moniker to mock his deformities and inability to fight back. But now, it was a badge of honor, a symbol of his transformation into something more powerful.

The moonlight cast a pale aura over the scene inside the cabin, highlighting the fear on Mary and Shelly's faces. Smash-Mouth's upper lip curled into a mutilated half-smile. He relished their abject fear and how their hands trembled as they turned the locking fasteners on all the portals into and out of the cabin. It was a far cry from the confident, carefree girls he remembered from high school. They had changed, but so had he.

He was once Jimmy Smazmoth, a boy with dreams and hopes. He had wanted nothing more than to fit in, to be accepted. But those dreams had been shattered by the pertinacious cruelty of his peers. Now, he was a specter of vengeance who had returned to reclaim what he was owed. He felt a perverse satisfaction. They were scrambling to protect themselves, but he would let them waste their spirit on this task, for he knew it was futile. There was no escape from the reckoning he had brought upon them. Finally, he had the power to make them pay.

The sight of Mary and Shelly, so close yet so vulnerable, ignited a thrill in his chest. He imagined the looks in their eyes when they realized he was not just a figment of their nightmares but an actual, imminent threat. The anticipation of their screams, their pleas for mercy, sent a wave of exhilaration through his whole body.

As the moments stretched into a delectable eternity, Smash-Mouth allowed himself to savor the impending climax of his long-fought vendetta. The night glow glinted off the glass, casting eerie reflections that settled in his eyes. He took a deep breath, the cold night air filling his lungs, and prepared to make his move.

Smash-Mouth clenched his fists, the sensation of his nails digging into his palms grounding him in the present. The past had shaped him, but it was the present that mattered now. The hunt, the chase, the ultimate confrontation—this was his moment. He was the predator, and they were his prey. The game was far from over, and he was determined to see it through to its end.

CHAPTER 30: THE IGNORANT BLISS

In the cozy bathroom, amidst the lively chatter of the drips of running water, Linda remained blissfully unaware of the storm brewing outside. She stood before the sink, dressed in her flannel pajamas. The soft fabric provided a comforting embrace against the chill of the night air but would undoubtedly serve little protection against a barbed football or a gridiron fist. She hummed a cheerful tune to herself, blissfully removed from the chaos unfolding downstairs. The melody, an old favorite from her childhood, brought a smile to her lips, starkly contrasting the mounting horror around her.

Linda turned on the tap, letting the warm water flow over her hands. She watched as the fake blood from earlier swirled down the drain, the crimson liquid the last physical marker of the ephemerality of the night's earlier antics. The séance, the jokes, the spooky atmosphere—they had all seemed like harmless fun at the time, but there seemed to be a cost. Not everyone had shared her enthusiasm for trickery. She chuckled softly, remembering how realistic the blood had looked and how they had all shrieked at the sight of her covered in it.

The warm water was soothing, a small luxury that Linda allowed herself to savor. She splashed her face, feeling the tension of the day beginning to melt away. The rhythmic sound of the water and the familiar routine of washing up provided a sense of normalcy that she desperately needed. In this small, steamy bolthole, the terrors of the night felt distant and unreal.

Linda's thoughts drifted to the weekend's original intent. She had looked forward to reconnecting with her old friends, reminiscing about their high school days, and creating new memories. The séance had been a fun idea, a way to add a little thrill to their gathering. She smiled at the thought of Shelly's enthusiasm and Mary's skeptical eye rolls. It was supposed to be just another adventure, a story they could laugh about for years. It hadn't gone well, but Linda doubted it was any kind of shortcoming in her performance that led to the unintended outcome.

As she dried her face with a soft towel, Linda's mind wandered to Deborah. She wondered if Deborah had been as spooked by the séance as she had pretended to be. Knowing Deborah, she had probably been rolling her eyes the whole time. Linda chuckled again at the thought. After all, Deborah was always the pragmatic voice of reason in their group.

Still oblivious to the grim reality outside the bathroom door, Linda took her time, enjoying the solitude. She brushed her teeth methodically, the minty freshness removing the lingering taste of the snacks they had shared earlier. She stared at her reflection in the mirror, noting the slight fatigue in her eyes.

She couldn't help but feel detached from the rest of the group. While she had noticed the strange atmosphere and Nancy and Mary's odd behavior, Linda had dismissed it as post séance jitters. She wasn't one to get easily rattled, and she had always prided herself on her level-headedness. The idea that something truly sinister was happening didn't quite register in her mind.

Linda's thoughts shifted to AJ and Jimmy Smazmoth. She remembered them from high school, but they were just faint memories, faces in the yearbook. The stories about Jimmy had always seemed exaggerated, the stuff of high school legend. She had never paid much attention to the rumors, focusing instead on her circle of friends and their teenage dramas.

Linda felt a sense of contentment as she rinsed her mouth and put her toothbrush away. The night had been full of surprises, but she was glad to be here with her friends, even if things hadn't gone exactly as planned. With the clarity of a clean face and minty fresh teeth, she now believed they would all laugh about this weekend in the future, forever sharing embellished tales of their spooky adventure with their friends and families.

CHAPTER 31: A MIND IN PARANOIA

Shelly's thoughts spiraled out of control, each more alarming than the last. Was Mary telling the truth, or could this be another retaliatory prank? The séance had gone poorly. Was Linda's alliance with Shelly justification enough for Mary to pull something like this? If the assassination of Franz Ferdinand could cause the world to collapse, why shouldn't a botched summoning lead to this stratagem?

Shelly navigated the game room, her movements quick and nervous. She looked around, checking under the pool table, behind furniture, and in every possible hiding place. She was briefly blinded by visions of AJ and Jimmy, the memories of high school blending with the horrors of the present. She shook it off and moved to the windows, ensuring each lock was secure.

At the same time, Mary moved through the living room, dining room, and into the kitchen, meticulously inspecting every window. She felt a moment of relief when she found them all secure. But that relief was short-lived. As she entered the kitchen, she stopped short, her eyes widening in horror. The back door was swung open, a calm night breeze blowing through the opening. Mary rushed to the door and closed it with a loud bang. She locked it and peered through the door portal, eyes scanning the outside. Her breath caught in her throat as she felt an eerie presence behind her.

Unbeknownst to her, Smash-Mouth had rushed by, his hulking form moving silently behind her. Mary spun around, her heart in her throat, but Smash-Mouth was gone, and she saw only Shelly turning the corner at the end of the hall.

"Everything secure?" Shelly inquired.

Mary nodded, trying to calm her racing heart. "Yeah. You?"

"All secure. Should we call the police?" Shelly replied.

Mary nodded and rushed to the phone, her fingers fumbling with the receiver. She pressed it to her ear, but there was no dial tone. Just silence. "You've got to be kidding me," she muttered, slamming the receiver down.

CHAPTER 32: THE DARKNESS FALLS

The cabin, once a cozy refuge, had transformed into a house of horrors as the night deepened. One by one, the lights in each room flickered and then went out, shifting the interior into a languid deviltry. The fireplace's warm glow, which had offered a semblance of comfort, dimmed and then extinguished, leaving the room bathed in a cold blue.

The sudden loss of light was a jarring contrast to the cozy ambiance that had previously filled the cabin. The once-welcoming living room, with its plush furniture and inviting decor, now seemed sinister and foreboding. The only light now came from the moon, casting inky patterns through the windows and highlighting the dust motes swirling in the air.

In the upstairs bathroom, Linda was blissfully unaware of the truculence descending upon the rest of the house. She hummed softly to herself, the familiar routine providing a momentary escape from the bizarre events of the evening. The light above her flickered and went out.

"Shit!" she exclaimed, startled by the sudden plunge into black. She fumbled for the light switch, flipping it up and down to no avail. Once a small sanctuary, the bathroom now felt claustrophobic and menacing in the absence of light. It was as if illumination was the only thread of joy gilding her dearth of hope. Underneath it all, Linda was a person of profound insecurity and deep regret.

Downstairs, Mary and Shelly were equally startled by the sudden blackout. The loss of illumination was so complete that it felt as if the air turned solid around them.

"Shelly!" Mary called out.

Shelly called up the stairs, "Linda, are you okay up there?"

"Yeah. What's with the lights?" Linda's voice drifted down, tinged with confusion but not yet alarm.

Mary's suspicions were growing. "Hey, Linda. Just be careful up there, okay?" she called, her tone serious.

Shelly tapped across the counter until she found and grabbed a flashlight. She lit it up, the beam cutting through with stark clarity. "We need to figure out what's going on," she said.

Linda stepped out of the bathroom. She muttered to herself, "So much for a relaxing weekend—" Her words were cut off as Smash-Mouth appeared suddenly, grabbing her with a force that knocked the breath out of her. She screamed, the sound sharp and filled with dread, but it was quickly silenced by a sickening gargle.

Mary and Shelly froze downstairs as Linda's scream bounced through the house. The sound cut off abruptly, replaced by a thud and an ominous silence.

"Linda?!" Shelly called out, crackling with fear. She shined the flashlight up the staircase, its beam piercing but revealing only an empty hallway.

Shelly started to ascend the stairs, but Mary grabbed her arm, pointing to the knives in the kitchen. They doubled back and each grabbed one, the cold steel offering a small measure of comfort against the unknown horrors awaiting them.

"I'll go check it out. Stay here," Shelly said, trying to sound braver than she felt.

"Like hell, I will," Mary stated firmly. They would face whatever was up there together.

Huddling close, Mary and Shelly crept up the dark staircase, their footsteps muffled by the thick carpet. Every creak of the carpeted wood gave them pause as their flashlight beams crawled along the walls.

The bathroom was empty, the mirror reflecting only their frightened faces. There was no sign of Linda, no indication of the atrocity that had just occurred. But then Mary's flashlight beam caught a glint on the floor—a maroon streak of blood. It led down the hallway toward Linda's room.

The door to Linda's room was closed, the blood trail disappearing beneath it. They exchanged a look of dread before slowly pushing the door open. Linda lay on the floor, her lifeless eyes staring blankly at the ceiling. A pool of blood surrounded her, the vivid red stark against the pale carpet. The room, which had been filled with laughter and camaraderie only hours before, was now a scene of unimaginable horror.

Mary and Shelly both reacted instinctively, backing out of the room in shock. They turned and rushed back into the hallway, their minds struggling to process the reality.

As they headed toward the stairs, Mary's frantic flashlight beam caught something that made her blood run cold—Smash-Mouth's deformed face. He was waiting for them, a manifestation of their deepest fears.

In an instant, he swung his lethal football wrapped in barbed wire, aiming directly at Mary's ankle. The impact was brutal, sending a jolt of pain shooting up her leg and causing her to collapse with a scream. The sound rattled the house, mingling with the creaks and groans of the old wood.

Desperation surged through Mary as she scrambled to regain her footing, but Smash-Mouth was ruthless. He grabbed her by the leg, dragging her down the stairs with terrifying ease. Her fingers clawed at the wooden steps, leaving bloody streaks as she struggled to resist his overpowering grip. Her nails cracked in half until she had no more spikes to lay a claim into the wood.

"Shelly! Help!" Mary's voice was raw and painful, and her pleas for help reverberated through the stairwell.

Shelly's flashlight beam cut through the confusion, her face stretched across her skull with horror as she witnessed Mary being dragged away. With a burst of adrenaline, she lunged forward, grabbing Mary's outstretched hand, trimmed with broken fingernails, in a desperate attempt to pull her back. The two women strained against Smash-Mouth's brutal strength, their clenches slipping and sliding against the blood-slicked wood.

"Hold on, Mary!" Shelly cried.

Smash-Mouth yanked Mary with a force that broke their control, sending her sprawling back into his clutches. Panic clawed at Mary's mind as she tried to twist free, but Smash-Mouth's grip was like iron. He raised his barbed football above his head, the vicious spikes glinting menacingly in the dim light.

Mary's survival instincts kicked in. She reached out, grabbing Smash-Mouth's wrist in a desperate attempt to deflect the blow. They were locked in a deadly struggle for a moment, Mary's eyes wide with fear and determination, Smash-Mouth's eyes filled with a sadistic exuberance.

Smash-Mouth wrenched his arm free with a snarl and brought the football down with devastating force. The first blow landed with a sickening thud, the razors cutting deep into the flesh of Mary's face. She had worked so hard to stay beautiful for all these years. The razors slid across her cheekbone, rending the flesh from her skull. She cried out in agony, her screech bursting through the house like a death knell. Blow after blow rained down on her, each one sapping more of her strength and decorticating more of her crown, her cries growing weaker with each movement.

"Stop!" Mary gasped.

But there was no mercy in Smash-Mouth's eyes. He continued his assault, the football rising and falling in an unrestrained, callous rhythm. Blood and tissue splattered across the stairs, the brutal scene illuminated by the flickering flashlight beams.

Smash-Mouth raised the football one ultimate time and brought it down with a sickening thud. Mary's body went limp, her final breath escaping in a gurgle as the last of her strength faded away.

Shelly crouched there in shock, tears streaming down her face. "Mary? Mary?!" she sobbed.

Smash-Mouth lifted his head, his eyes locking onto Shelly with a predatory gaze. "Touchdown!" he snarled, his voice twisting with malice.

Shelly screamed. She turned, ran up the stairs, and darted into her room, slamming the door behind her. She pressed her back against the door, trying to catch her breath.

Shelly's mind raced, her thoughts a chaotic whirlpool of fear and desperation. She could hardly believe what she had just witnessed. Her friend torn apart by a monster wearing the guise of a man. The horror of it all seemed surreal like Grand Guignol theater being performed before her eyes. As she tried to steady her breathing, memories from recent years flooded back, times when the world seemed to make more sense, when the future was something bright to look forward to, not a nightmare to escape.

She remembered the summer of love, the music festivals, the protests against an unjust war that seemed endless. She recalled the faces of friends lost in the struggle for peace, the hope that had once filled her heart. Now, that hope seemed like a distant whimper, a faint glimmer doused by the screams of her friends and the malevolent laughter of Smash-Mouth.

Shelly's mind wandered to the nights spent under the stars, sharing dreams and fears with those who believed in a better world. The smell of incense and the sound of acoustic guitars played by campfires filled her senses. She longed for that simplicity, for the days when their biggest worry was which record to play next. But those days were replaced by a reality too cruel to fathom.

Despite the terror gripping her, Shelly felt a fierce determination igniting. She could not let Mary's death be in vain. She thought of the women who had come before her, faced impossible odds, and still found the strength to fight. Now a tomb of horror, this cabin could not be where their story ended.

The songs of rebellion, love, and defiance filled her thoughts, blending with the adrenaline coursing through her veins.

Giocoso!

Appassionato!

The optimism she had once merely feigned had gradually taken root in her over the recent years. Now, though dimmed, it was not entirely extinguished. Shelly resolved to channel that spirit and use it as a shield against the encroaching nothing.

With every fiber of her being, she vowed to fight back. For Mary, for Linda, for Deborah, for Nancy, for Brenda, for all the dreams that had been shattered. She could feel the strength of her generation behind her, pushing her forward, reminding her that even in the face of overwhelming darkness, there was always a glimmer of light. She would not be defeated. Not tonight. Not ever.

CHAPTER 33: THE LAST STAND

With the enemy closing in, Shelly knew this would be her final stand. Outside the door, Smash-Mouth's footsteps grew louder, each stomp a harbinger of doom. Shelly's psyche was fractured. She panicked in a chaotic whirlwind of fear and desperation. She knew she had to find a way to stay calm. She had to find a way to survive. As she played out every possible scenario in her head, she did not see a clear path to safety, let alone victory.

The pounding on the other side was immediate and furious, each blow sending convulsions through the door frame. Shelly desperately searched for somewhere to hide.

Hopelessness clawed at her as she scanned the space. Her eyes fell on the sliding terrace doors. She flung them open, the cool night air rushing in, but then hesitated. That would have been too obvious a move. Instead, she left the terrace doors open but ducked into the closet, hoping it would throw Smash-Mouth off the trail. She closed the closet door just enough to conceal her hiding place while leaving a sliver of visibility.

The door to the bedroom burst open with a crash, and Smash-Mouth stormed in. His elephantine form loomed in the dim light, shaking with a manic rage. He heaved and roared before freezing in the center of the room. He moved with predatory precision, checking under the bed first, then methodically searching the rest of the room. He approached the closet, and Shelly's breath caught in her throat. She could see his shadow through the small gap in the door.

As he reached for the closet, his eyes flicked to the open terrace doors. Assuming his prey had escaped to the outside, he turned and stepped slowly and deliberately onto the terrace. He had done just what Shelly had hoped for. Shelly watched him disappear into the night. Her heart pounded as she counted the seconds, waiting for the perfect moment to make her move.

Seizing her chance, Shelly silently slipped out of the closet and darted for the door. Her adrenaline-fueled movements were swift but quiet. She glanced back once, just in time to see Smash-Mouth re-enter the room, catching her escape in a mirror. Having realized his mistake, he played along, acting as though he had seen nothing. He stood still, scanning the room with the intensity and patience of a lion on the hunt.

Shelly crept into the hallway, relieved that she made such a narrow escape. The silence was so oppressive that every creak and groan of the old house exploded in her ears. She peered back one more time into the bedroom, her heart sinking as she saw it was empty.

"Oh, no," she mouthed inaudibly.

She tensed as she contemplated her next move. The silence stretched on, each second feeling like an eternity. She could feel Smash-Mouth creeping closer, the danger palpable.

Suddenly, a floorboard creaked behind her. Shelly turned sharply. Smash-Mouth loomed over her, his gnarled face inches from hers, his dead eyes filled with malevolent intent. He swung his football, but Shelly ducked, the razors wrapped around the ball jammed into the wall with a sickening thud.

She took off running, her feet barely touching the ground as she fled down the staircase. As she looked back to determine whether Smash-Mouth was tailing her, she nearly stumbled over Mary's lifeless body. The sight of her friend's brutalized form renewed her resolve, and her breath sharpened. Behind her, Smash-Mouth roared in fury, his footsteps pounding in pursuit.

As she reached the room below, she shouted up the stairs to show her strength. She had heard once that if you encountered a coyote or bear in the wild, it was better to yell at them than to run. She wasn't sure if that was true, and even if it was, she really wasn't sure if the sample principle might apply in this case, but she had little to lose. "Leave me alone! I never did anything to you!" Shelly screamed at Smash-Mouth, but he hastened toward her.

She flailed and kicked and punched at him, her fear giving her strength. His football swung through the air and scraped her arm, the razors slicing through her skin. She winced but didn't stop.

"Touchdown!" Smash-Mouth growled.

Shelly grabbed a wine bottle from a nearby table and smashed it across his head. The impact staggered him, but he recovered quickly, his eyes burning with the hunt. She grabbed another bottle and hit him again, harder this time. He roared in pain, the glass shattering and embedding shards into his flesh. His eyes stung with slivers of glass sticking out of his corneas.

Taking advantage of his momentary disorientation, Shelly dashed toward the front door. She flung it open and raced outside into the night, her feet pounding against the dirt path. The wind whipped at her hair and clothes, but she didn't slow down. She could hear Smash-Mouth's furious roar behind her, but this time, she didn't dare to look back.

CHAPTER 34: NANCY IN WHITE

This has become the story of what a woman's patience can endure and what a man's resolution to evil can achieve. AJ imagined that his legend and the legend of Smash-Mouth would be passed on through rumor and insinuation, just as it had been thus far. But this time, it would not just be a story of one fateful moment on the timeline of a high school, but one fateful legend on the timeline of man.

Nancy sat in the chair, her hands bound tightly, her body trembling with a mixture of fear and revulsion. Unlike AJ, she was much more practical and focused on the issue at hand rather than how history might view this moment should its likely conclusion come to fruition. For Nancy, the likelihood of any conclusion was irrelevant to her determination and dedication to a repeat of her miraculous survival. That would be Nancy's myth, and she would be just fine if that story died in this shack's putrid walls rather than on the aging, cracked lips of long-forgotten gossips.

Dried blood and chunks of flesh clung to her chin and clothes, remnants of the vile concoction she had been forced to ingest. She felt nauseous, on the verge of being sick at any moment, but she fought to keep herself together. Her eyes, wide with horror, stared at her captor.

"Why are you doing this?" she asked, feeling hopeless.

AJ, standing over a gruesome array of body parts and blood-stained tools, looked at her with a chilling calmness. "I won't bore you with details you haven't earned."

Nancy tried to gain an understanding of the madness. "You kill people. I get it."

"Jimmy's gotta eat," AJ replied nonchalantly.

"Oh, god," Nancy wailed, her stomach churning.

AJ chuckled darkly. "The Smazmoths took me in when no one else would. I looked out for Jimmy like he was my own brother. Kept him safe."

As he spoke, AJ stirred a glass of bloody puree with a rusty spoon, the sound raising goosebumps and making Nancy's skin crawl. "People mock those they don't understand. Jimmy had goals and dreams just like everybody else."

"I never mocked Jimmy," Nancy protested, desperation creeping in.

AJ's eyes flashed with anger. "You ignored him. You didn't give a rat's ass about Jimmy Smazmoth until your friends started getting what they deserved."

Nancy's heart ached with guilt and fear. "You've won then. They're all dead. Jimmy's been avenged. It's over."

AJ's response was swift and violent. He hurled the bloody glass against the wall, shattering it into bits. "No, see, that's where you're wrong! It's the legend of Smash-Mouth, Nancy. We're just getting started."

He pointed to a pile of bones and clothing, all that was left of Deborah and the backwoods creep. "Bullies everywhere will think twice when word gets out. This isn't just about high school. It's after high school. It's life, Nancy."

Nancy remained stoic, her mind reeling with the realization of the horror that surrounded her.

AJ's voice trembled with rage. "You people broke his goddamn jaw! He can't eat or live like anyone else!"

AJ picked up a cleaver and swung it around, emphasizing his words. "It's so easy for you all to forget those you torment and move on."

Nancy's eyes filled with tears. "I haven't moved on! None of us have! That's why we're here! I am so sorry for what I've done. I'm sorry for what we all did. We can't change the past."

AJ's expression hardened. "This is about the future now. That quiet kid getting picked on for being different. People are horrible. You know this is true."

He stepped over to the blender, flicking it on. The blades whirred menacingly. "You get to live your lives like regular people. You get to eat like regular people. We're here to shake things up."

AJ grabbed Nancy's arm, raising her sleeve. "You are the main course, after all," he said, slowly cutting into her arm.

Nancy screamed and squirmed in the chair, her mind overwhelmed with pain and fear. A sudden thump against the shack door made AJ stop cutting.

"Jimmy?" AJ called out.

Another thump came from the side wall. AJ's frustration was evident as he rolled his eyes and turned off the blender. The dramatic moment had been broken. "Jimmy, you back?"

He crept over to the door, opening it slightly. The leaves crackled beneath someone's feet outside. AJ turned swiftly, his eyes narrowing.

Suddenly, Shelly appeared from around the corner of the shack, hammer in hand. With a determined cry, she swung it at AJ's head. The impact sent him reeling, his head banging against the shack door as he fell unconscious.

Shelly let out a breath, amazed that her plan had worked. She dropped the hammer and grabbed the cleaver from the slab. She quickly cut the ropes binding Nancy to the chair.

"Come on, Shelly. Let's go," Nancy urged as she grabbed a knife from the nearby shelf.

But Shelly took a moment to observe the interior and the piles of body parts. "Poor Deb," she added, covering her mouth in shock.

Before they could move, AJ came back to awareness. He leaped toward them, missing and falling to the ground, still dizzy from the head injury. Blood poured down his face.

AJ grabbed Nancy's leg, pulling her back. There was a fierce struggle, and Nancy put all her will and might into it. But alas, Nancy was unable to break free. A gust of wind slammed the creaky shack door shut, cutting them all off from the forest air.

Shelly's eyes focused intently on AJ's leg as he held onto Nancy with a grip like a steel trap. The cleaver in her hand felt both heavy and empowering, a tool of desperation turned into a weapon of survival. With a burst of adrenaline, she swung the cleaver down with all the strength she could muster.

The blade connected with AJ's leg just below the knee, emitting a sickening thud. The impact jarred her arms, sending vibrations through her arm muscles, but she held firm. Blood erupted from the wound in an abundant spray, splattering onto the ground and across her clothes. AJ's scream, raw and guttural, filled the air, a visceral response to the sudden, brutal injury.

Shelly didn't stop. She raised the cleaver again, her determination unwavering despite the horror of the act. She brought it down a second time, the blade biting deeper into flesh and bone. The sound was turbulent, a mix of crunching and slicing that seemed to clamor in the stillness of the night.

AJ's leg began to give way, the bones cracking under the rapid assault. With each swing, the cleaver cleaved through sinew and muscle, severing the limb further until it was barely attached. Blood pooled around them, the once strong leg now a mangled mess of tissue and shattered bone.

With a final, powerful strike, Shelly brought the blade down straight through, severing the leg completely. AJ howled in agony, the pain overwhelming him as he clutched at the bloody stump. The severed leg fell to the ground with a dull thud. The cleaver, now slick with blood, hung heavy in Shelly's hand, the gravity of her actions sinking in even as she prepared for what came next.

The door burst open, and Smash-Mouth rushed in, catching Shelly off guard. She swung the cleaver at him, but he was quicker, slashing her with his football.

"Touchdown! Woo-hoo!" Smash-Mouth shouted with delectation.

"Jimmy!" Nancy called out desperately.

Smash-Mouth stopped, captivated by his former crush.

"That's right, Jimmy. It's me, Nancy. You remember, right?" she said in the most soothing tone she could muster.

Jimmy's terrible eyes softened, and he reached out to touch her. It was the first gentle touch he had given or received since his mother died.

"It's all over now, Jimmy. You can stop this," Nancy continued calmly.

Jimmy dropped the football and moved closer toward her. In a swift move, taking advantage of Jimmy having let his guard down, Nancy slashed his hand and forearm with the knife. He stumbled back, clutching his arm.

Nancy and Shelly took off running, their breathing rapid and their hearts pounding. They had to survive. They had to end this madness once and for all. Smash-Mouth followed close behind.

AJ lay on the cold ground, his body convulsing in pain. His face, contorted in a grimace of sheer agony, was pale and slick with sweat. Blood poured from the stump where his leg had been, the viscous fluid pooling beneath him and staining the earth a dark crimson. His hands, trembling and slick with his own blood, clutched at the severed limb, futilely trying to staunch the flow.

The raw, exposed flesh of the stump was a horrific sight, muscles and tendons frayed and torn, with splintered bone jutting out. Each throb of his heart sent another spurt of blood into the air, the life force draining from him with sickening pulsing. The severed nerves screamed with pain, sending searing waves of torment through his body.

AJ inhaled hard, followed by exhales that sounded like whimpering moans. He tried to speak, but only guttural, unintelligible sounds emerged, his voice lost to the depths of his pain.

The bloody stump waved weakly in the air, a gory flag of his defeat and desperation. His body shuddered forcefully, the agony overwhelming his senses and blurring the edges of his consciousness. Each involuntary twitch of the severed limb sent new jolts of pain shooting through him, his mind barely able to comprehend the full extent of his injury.

AJ's entire existence had been reduced to this singular, excruciating moment, the world around him fading as he failed to fulfill his brutal destiny.

CHAPTER 35: THE LAST OF THE GUARDIANS

It was a feature peculiar to the colonial wars of North America, that the toils and dangers of the wilderness were to be encountered before the adverse hosts could meet. The ripples of this peculiarity crossed the minds of the escapees as they stumbled over branches and found their shoes caught in mud or moss with each trudging step of their sprints. Nancy and Shelly ran for their lives. Behind them, Smash-Mouth's shocking silhouette lurched through the underbrush, his movements more erratic and desperate than before. Still, he seemed unperturbed by his injury and the physical obstacles of the woods. His voice, anfractuous with madness, thundered through the trees.

"Touchdown!" he screamed, his tone a chilling blend of triumph and insanity. Each shout was a reminder of the brutal violence he was capable of, propelling the runners forward with even greater urgency.

Nancy's lungs burned with each craggy breath. She could hear Shelly's footsteps just ahead, a comforting reminder that she was not alone in this nightmare. They weaved through the trees, ducking under low branches and leaping over fallen logs, their movements frantic and uncoordinated.

The ground was uneven, roots and rocks jutting out treacherously. Nancy stumbled but managed to keep her balance, her heart pounding not just from exertion but from the sheer terror coursing through her veins.

Behind them, Smash-Mouth's heavy footfalls were growing louder, his misshapen form moving with a terrifying speed. Nancy could almost feel his breath on the back of her neck, the proximity of danger making her push past the limits of her endurance. The forest seemed endless, an unforgiving expanse that offered no immunity, only the promise of more horror if they slowed down for even a moment.

On the trail, Shelly suddenly stopped, gripping the cleaver tightly. Nancy, a few steps ahead, turned back, her confusion evident. "Shelly, what are you doing?" she asked.

"Keep running. I'll hold him off for as long as possible," Shelly replied, determined.

"No! Come with me, Shelly. Please. We can make it," Nancy pleaded, her eyes wide with fear and desperation.

Shelly shook her head, a sad smile on her face. "Someone has to tell the story."

"But—" Nancy began, but Shelly cut her off.

"Go. I've got some fight left," Shelly insisted.

They embraced tightly. "It was a lovely and healing retreat," Nancy said through a mixture of smiles and tears.

They shared a bittersweet laugh, knowing this might be the end. Smash-Mouth's footsteps grew louder, danger closing in.

"Go, Nancy," Shelly urged, pushing her away gently.

With one last look back, Nancy took off running.

CHAPTER 36: THE THIN YELLOW LINE

A hundred and fifty yards away, a little to the right, Shelly saw a motionless man, arms in the form of a touchdown signal, standing on the bare open hillside. The statuesque silhouette could have honored a fallen school comrade in stone, but she knew this was no sculpture. This was a living graven image. The monstrosity returned to life from its brazen pose and moved into the tree line and toward her. He had apparently locked onto her scent.

Shelly hid behind a tree, her heart pounding as she listened to the approaching footsteps. The silence between each step was unbearable. He grew closer.

Smash-Mouth ran past Shelly's hiding spot but quickly stopped short, sensing her behind him. He slowly turned to face her, his teratoid jaw hanging loose. He was breathing heavily from the pursuit, but unlike most who might open wider for a deeper, more voluminous gasp of air, Smash-Mouth's jaw remained forever open, forever allowing him to draw gusts inward to fuel the cursed mission thrust upon him by the Donner High football team and his doting mother. The deformity made him a living nightmare, an oddity that chilled Shelly to her core, but it also aided his ability to take in air.

With a burst of courage, Shelly emerged from behind the tree. "Gimme an F. Gimme a U. Gimme a FUCK YOU!" she yelled defiantly. She charged at Smash-Mouth, ramming into his belly like a linebacker. They tumbled to the ground, and Shelly slashed at him repeatedly with her cleaver.

Smash-Mouth retaliated, catching her in the side with his football, dragging the razors across her belly. Shelly screamed in pain, but she continued to fight, her desperation fueling her strength.

Smash-Mouth's eyes gleamed with a maniacal light, his asymmetric smile widening as he relished the taste of Shelly's defiance. The sounds of their struggle trumpeted through the forest in a warped symphony of pain and fury. Smash-Mouth's immense frame loomed over Shelly as he prepared to deliver another crushing blow.

Shelly, despite the searing pain in her side, refused to relent. She slashed at Smash-Mouth's face, her cleaver finding purchase in his dripping jaw. Blood sprayed, and he howled in agony, the sound reverberating through the trees like a banshee's wail. His rage intensified, and he swung wildly, trying to dislodge her.

The two combatants rolled across the twigs and leaves, their bodies tangled in an intemperate pas de deux. Shelly's determination was unyielding; She had faced down police batons and tear gas, and she would face down this monstrosity, too. Each memory fueled her resolve, turning her fear into a burning fury.

Smash-Mouth's brute strength was overwhelming, but Shelly's agility and tenacity kept her in the fight. She ducked and weaved, avoiding his crushing blows by a hair's breadth.

As they struggled, the forest seemed to close in around them, the trees bearing silent witness to their savage grapple. The moonlight filtering through the canopy revealed the raw desperation embossed into Shelly's features and Smash-Mouth's evil joy.

With a primal scream, Shelly drove her cleaver into Smash-Mouth's shoulder, the blade biting deep into muscle and bone. He roared in pain, the sound shaking the leaves on the trees. But he did not falter. With a vicious swipe, he knocked the cleaver from her hand, sending it skittering across the forest floor.

Unarmed and bleeding, Shelly's eyes darted around, searching for anything she could use as a weapon. Her gaze locked onto a jagged rock, partially buried in the dirt. With a surge of adrenaline, she lunged for it, grabbing the rough stone and swinging it at Smash-Mouth with all her might. The rock connected with his temple, and he staggered back, momentarily dazed.

Seizing the opportunity, Shelly scrambled to her feet, her breaths coming in stuttered gasps. Blood dripped from her wounds, staining the ground beneath her. She could feel her strength waning, but she refused to give up. Smash-Mouth advanced toward her again, shaking off the stun, his eyes blazing with murderous intent.

Shelly backed up against a tree, her vision blurring from blood loss. She knew she had only one chance left. Summoning every ounce of strength she had left, she hurled the rock at Smash-Mouth's head. It struck him squarely in the forehead, and he collapsed to the ground with a guttural growl.

The forest was silent for a moment except for Shelly's labored breathing. She watched as Smash-Mouth lay motionless, her heart pounding in her chest. Had she done it? Had she finally defeated the monster that had haunted their lives?

But then, with a low, menacing groan, Smash-Mouth began to stir. He pushed himself up on one arm, his eyes locking onto Shelly with a hatred that burned through the air. Shelly's heart sank, knowing this fight was far from over.

Desperation fueled her next move. She grabbed a fallen branch, brandishing it like a spear. As Smash-Mouth rose to his feet, Shelly charged, driving the branch into his chest with all her might. The improvised weapon pierced his flesh, and he barked again in agony.

But even impaled, Smash-Mouth refused to fall. He clawed at the branch, trying to dislodge it, his strength undiminished by the wound. With her energy spent, Shelly could do nothing but watch as the monster before her continued to fight.

At that moment, the night seemed to hold its breath, and Shelly realized the true horror of their situation.

Smash-Mouth was not just a man. He was a force of nature, an embodiment of vengeance and pain that could not be easily vanquished. And as long as he drew breath, their nightmare would never end.

CHAPTER 37: THE DEER SLAYER

On the human imagination, events produce the effects of time. Thus, she who has traveled far and seen much is apt to fancy that she has lived long enough. Nancy stopped running, her heart sinking as she heard Shelly's scream in the distance. Tears streamed down her face as she backed against a tree, trying to stay hidden. She needed to think of her next move, but her mind was a whirlwind of fear and dejection.

Maybe she had outrun the specter of death too long, and inevitability had arrived. She almost wished it had happened fifteen years sooner, but if today was to be the day, she might believe that those years were the era of limbo before she finally made her descent into the underworld.

Nancy truly believed in an afterlife after the séance and her possession, but she doubted she lived a life righteous enough to deserve a different fate than Angela, who served both as her tormentor and her victim.

Perhaps that was Angela's sinister plan all along, slay those who destroyed her son's body and damn the one who poisoned her son's mind with unrequited adulation.

Nancy looked around, searching for any sign of escape. It was all trees, dirt, and dark. Then, through the stillness, she heard the faint sound of a truck's engine—a large motor sound in the distance.

Without hesitation, Nancy took off in that direction, her hope rekindled. But before she could reach safety, Smash-Mouth lunged from the blackness, attacking her with brutal force. She recoiled from the sight of his sinisterly warped face, and before she could break the trance and act, he threw her to the ground.

"Touchdown!" he screamed, staging a macabre celebration. He clutched his football, ready to strike.

As Smash-Mouth raised his weapon, Nancy acted on pure instinct. She kicked him in the testicles with all her might. Smash-Mouth wailed in pain, dropped his football, and collapsed.

Nancy grabbed the football, her hands trembling. She stood over Smash-Mouth, who writhed in pain at her feet. With a surge of rage and determination, she slammed the football down on him, driving it into his head.

Blood oozed down over his face, and he stopped moving. Nancy stared at him, her breath shallow. She kicked his leg to be sure he was dead, then backed away, her mind reeling.

Nancy looked around, trying to remember the right direction. Her body ached, and her mind was exhausted, but she knew she had to keep moving. With a final glance at Smash-Mouth's lifeless body, she took off running again, determined to survive the night and tell the story of the conditions they had endured.

CHAPTER 38: THE GREAT NANCY

In Nancy's younger and more vulnerable years, her father gave her some advice that she has been turning over in her mind ever since. "Whenever you feel like criticizing anyone," he told her, "just remember that all the people in this world haven't had the advantages that you've had."

For over twenty-five years, this mantra was repeated in her head, but she had yet to find a way to apply it to anything of a practical nature. Perhaps there would never be a practical mapping for such a platitudinous concept, but she could never shake the idea. One might describe its emergence at this moment as inappropriate, but if you've ever faced death and gazed into his voidsome eyes, tasting his cold breath in your own mouth, the most unlikely regrets and unsolved puzzles would cross your mind, too.

While the application may be improbable or impossible, Nancy found it justification to suddenly mourn both Angela and Jimmy and the circumstances under which she was compelled to terminate them. Any ethicist would side with her, she argued to herself, but she could not shake the feeling that morality could never be so cut and dry. To kill rather than to die under such threats may still yield a judgment of damnation in the eyes of a higher being.

This realization chilled Nancy, and she held her breath for many moments too long in its wake. When she returned to the present challenge in lieu of facing an imagined tribunal on her deeds, her lungs burned as she sprinted through the dense forest, dodging hanging tree branches and leaping over fallen bark that littered her path. Every step was a struggle, her legs aching from the relentless pace. She burst through the last line of trees and found herself in a clearing that led to the main road.

She smiled to herself, a flicker of hope igniting in her chest. She didn't dare look back, maintaining a steady pace on the empty pavement. The road stretched out before her like a promise of salvation, each step taking her further from the nightmare she had just escaped.

Morning light filtered through the trees, casting a serene glow over the landscape. Nancy had found a spot under a large oak tree, and exhaustion had finally claimed her. She collapsed and almost immediately slept soundly, the peaceful silence of the morning a stark contrast to the chaos of the previous night.

The sudden roar of a car engine jolted her awake. Disoriented, she looked around, trying to get her bearings. The car that had just zoomed by was already a distant speck on the horizon. Panic surged through her as she scrambled to her feet and ran to the side of the road.

"Hey! Please help me! Come back!" she shouted, waving her arms frantically. But the car was too far gone, its driver oblivious to her plight.

Silence enveloped her once more as she stood by the road, alone with her thoughts. She began to walk, each step heavy, dragging a ball and chain of despair. Tears threatened to spill, but she fought them back, determined to keep moving.

Suddenly, a rustling noise from behind caught her attention. Before she could react, Smash-Mouth lunged from the woods, his grotesque form even more horrifying in the daylight. The wire from his football was stuck in his head, blood oozing down his face. He grunted angrily, his eyes filled with a murderous rage.

He grabbed Nancy with a vice-like grip, lifting her off the ground. She kicked and screamed, but her struggles were in vain. Smash-Mouth dragged her back into the woods, the promise of the road and the fleeting glimmer of hope fading behind her.

As another approaching car passed by, oblivious to the scene unfolding just beyond the tree line, the forest swallowed Nancy's screams, leaving only a haunting silence behind. One of the most peculiar things about nature is its deference to context. That same tree might be a wondrous gift from God when it provides shade on a calm, hot summer day. That same tree could instead beckon lightning on a stormy night. Its branches might crack and tumble, crushing every living thing below it. Even without such dramatic external events, such a tree had been Nancy's place of rest and solace just before her apparently unextinguishable rival leaped from behind its mighty trunk to overwhelm her.

The profundity did not elude Nancy, for while she had told Deborah that she had been only thinking for the past 15 years, she neglected to mention her fervent consumption of philosophical texts. Her primary goal in this pursuit was to understand whether her taking of

Angela's life was a morally justifiable act in the context of the situation.

Like a tree, she believed a person was neither inherently good nor evil, but that personhood is only a neutral state in which context and meaning play essential roles in ethical puzzles. She had read Wittgenstein and Frege, preferring the former over the latter but finding that neither brought her closer to a resolution of her ethical conundrums.

Nancy was not necessarily a theist, but as with virtually all Western Culturists, she feared that ethical failure could lead to some form of damnation. There was enough talk of such a place or thing across religions throughout the centuries. She occasionally fell back on the Judeo-Christian Bible to make the auto-argument that Exodus presented law consistent with the Hammurabian eye for an eye postulate. She never could quite reconcile this with the abutting Pentateuchal passages, which told in great detail how slaves should be legally handled in a retributive justice context, not for enslavement, but rather for any physical injury they might endure.

Perhaps she had studied too many philosophical perspectives and failed to adopt the traditional academic policy of declaring that the one most convenient to a quandary is the most correct. This had become so common on college campuses at the time that it almost felt part of a standardized curriculum.

Since Nancy had no formal education, she was not privy to this standard and thus remained vexed.

CHAPTER 39: HEART OF DARKNESS

Nancy's eyes fluttered open, her vision gradually adjusting to the oppressive light that filled the room. The first sensation she registered was a tingling numbness in her right leg. Panic surged through her as she attempted to move, only to find herself securely bound to a heavy, wooden chair. With mounting horror, she gazed down at the limb. It was swollen and gangrenous looking. It had been bandaged in the middle. The wrap must have been too tight because she felt no sensation below the thigh.

Disoriented, Nancy's mind flashed back to her last moments of consciousness. She recalled the sensation of being anesthetized during dental surgery, the dentist's face a lifeless cardboard cutout. Her thoughts blurred, and she looked down at the leg again, gaining clarity and insight into the situation. She slowly realized with sickening dread that the leg there wasn't hers anymore—it was AJ's. Her leg had been severed and replaced with his, the two partials bound together with cloth.

In disbelief, her eyes scanned the room, her heart lodged in her throat. She realized she was in Shelly's cabin in that same cozy room of reminiscence from the night before.

As her visual field focused, space revealed the lifeless forms of Shelly, Mary, Linda, and Deborah, their pallid faces stark against the furnishings, sickeningly propped up in chairs near her. The sight was almost unbearable, and she choked up vomit.

In the corner, Smash-Mouth's face lit up. He clapped his hands together and sang in a horrifyingly cheerful voice, "Touchdown! Touchdown! Oh, we're scoring tonight!"

AJ stood at the head of the large wooden table, which had been moved into the center of the space. He carved into a roasted leg. The sickly sweet aroma that wafted through the air made Nancy's stomach churn. She retched, desperately trying to turn her face away from the distressing scene.

"Ah, Nancy," AJ began, slicing a piece of meat from the roasted leg and popping it into his mouth. His teeth gleamed eerily in the room's dim light. "You have no idea how delicious you are." He stood, propping himself up with a bleached femur cane to replace his missing leg. He hobbled toward her and placed a plate in front of her. It took Nancy a moment to realize that this was her leg, roasted to infernal perfection.

The realization sent her reeling, a scream building up in her throat. But before she could utter a sound, AJ held a forkful of meat to her lips. "Open up, Nancy. You must be starving!" he jeered.

She clamped her mouth shut, her eyes wide with terror. AJ plied his face into a Mephistophelian smirk. "Oh, come on now. It's just a taste of what's to come."

In the background, Smash-Mouth continued his profane dance, shouting with glee, "Touchdown! Touchdown!" The execratory scene was a nightmare come to life, and Nancy's heart slammed, every fiber of her being yearning to escape.

Nancy could not accept reality. Her mind drifted from this unthinkable truth as AJ force-fed Nancy slices of her own leg and then bits of Shelly, Mary, Linda, and finally Deborah to Nancy. She gagged and spit and fought back until her resolve was drained. AJ's patience and determination could certainly outlast her will, particularly as she was lightheaded from blood loss.

Eventually, she swallowed, accepting the hopelessness of this battle in a greater war. Nancy was very hungry; this meat was the best she had ever tasted.

As the evening wore on, Nancy became wholly disengaged from her mouth and her digestive tract. There was a tiny compartment of her intellect that held to humor in these scenarios of severe trauma and distress, situations she had become increasingly numb to.

In this small pocket of her mind, the phrase, "You are what you eat," kicked about, first as an ironic joke but finally emerging as an empowering principle. She may have been the last survivor of her Donner High friends, but through this imposed consumption, rumination, and ultimately digestion, Nancy had become an amalgamation of her companions. This line of thinking would be unlikely to continue in a sane mind, but extreme exhaustion and atrocities do not weave a nest for sanity.

As Nancy pondered whether her body remained her own in a Ship of Theseus parable, the philosophical musings were deeply contrasted by the cacophony of Smash-Mouth's cheers and AJ's mocking laughter. While her inner voice remained focused on the moral boundaries of a life of victimization, outwardly, Nancy howled.

Eventually, as the howling continued, Nancy's screams and pleas became background noise, fading into the indifference of the night. Her hope for escape or rescue dwindled with every passing moment, and she felt a cold grip tighten around her heart.

In her disoriented state, Nancy tried to move her focus away from Plutarch and take in every detail in the physical space around her. The room felt larger and lonelier than before. It no longer glowed with the warmth of the fireplace, but starlight streamed weakly through the dirty glass panes of the windows across from her.

Every time she attempted to free herself, her binds only felt tighter. Her horror began to meld into determination as the minutes turned to hours. She waited patiently, allowing herself to be humiliated and giving AJ a sense of security and safety. It was enough that he let his guard down. AJ was momentarily distracted, basking in Smash-Mouth's hedonic celebration and occasionally throwing a mocking comment Nancy's way.

Even in her diminished state, Nancy was not without her resourcefulness. She knew she had to remain calm and observant. She spotted a piece of sharp, broken glass from the shattered wine bottle Shelly had previously wielded against Smash-Mouth lying on the floor just a few feet from her chair.

Utilizing the leg that remained, Nancy nudged the glass closer to her, trying to do so without attracting AJ's attention. It took what felt like dramatic hours, missing many times with her clumsy feet. Eventually, she grasped the shard with her toes and raised it slowly to her bound hands behind her back. The pain from her missing limb was immense, but she remained steadfast. She had previously experienced enough brushes with death to know that the improbable and maybe even the impossible were actually potentially attainable.

A new wave of hope surged as she worked the shard against her ropes. She had already lost so much to them, but she wouldn't let AJ and Smash-Mouth take any more from her. The ropes slowly frayed, the sharp glass biting into them and occasionally piercing her skin. But the sting of these fresh wounds was nothing compared to the pain of the loss of her friends and her determination to survive.

Suddenly, the front door burst open. Two figures entered the room—people Nancy didn't recognize. It was clear they were allies of AJ and Smash-Mouth. The pair had apparently started organizing a family of miscreants. One of the new arrivals carried a tray of tools, while the other pushed in a cart that held an old-fashioned gramophone. The former wore a mask of human skin, sewn together from several desecrated victims.

"Thought we'd provide some music for our little gathering," the one with the gramophone smirked, setting it up as a haunting melody began to play on a lacquer 78.

Nancy realized she was almost free, but with four foes, she really needed a distraction. Looking around desperately, she noticed that old chandelier hanging precariously above AJ. It was adorned with bones and spikes, adding to the room's deathly décor. She had remembered looking at it upon arrival and finding it grim. Now, it was her only hope.

Utilizing the glass shard, she reflected a light beam toward the chandelier's chain. As it gleamed brightly, it caught Smash-Mouth's attention. "Shiny!" he exclaimed, moving closer to it. He leaped upward, grabbing at the illumination. The chain, weakened over the years, gave way, and the heavy chandelier crashed down, narrowly missing AJ but pinning Smash-Mouth underneath.

The room plunged into chaos. AJ screamed in rage. The newcomers scrambled to aid Smash-Mouth, and Nancy's binds finally gave way in the confusion. Taking a deep breath, she mustered all her strength and made a hopping dash for the basement stairs, using AJ's severed leg as a makeshift support and grabbing onto anything within reach to stay upright.

Heading down to the basement was risky, as she was unsure what the escape plan might be after that, but there was no unobstructed path to the front door nor the sliding doors out to the patio, so the basement was the only option. As she bounced down the stairs, she could hear the enraged shouts of AJ echoing behind her.

When she reached the bottom of the stairs, she was surprised to find a narrow path through shelves full of dried goods rather than a sprawling room. The maze of corridors looked endless, but Nancy's determination propelled her forward. She constantly stumbled and tripped over debris, her injured leg causing her immense pain. But the thought of freedom kept her going.

Suddenly, she found herself in front of a large metal door with a wheel. Taking a risk, she turned the wheel and pushed the door open. The stars greeted her. She had emerged from an underground bunker into a dense forest. She vaguely remembered that Shelly had mentioned that her family had built a fallout shelter under the cabin, and this was what she had stumbled upon.

While the two newcomers did pursue her, bloodhounds they were not. She had hidden in a bush, knowing she could not outrun them. Luckily, the pursuers rushed off into the woods following what they thought was her trail, but it was actually the carved path that Deborah's body had been dragged through earlier in the night. Nancy held her breath as they ran off.

Although exhausted, she knew she couldn't stop. Using the trees as cover, she hobbled away from the nightmare that had imprisoned her, still propped on AJ's leg. As she ventured deeper into the woods, she hoped she was heading toward civilization and prayed that AJ, Smash-Mouth, and their acolytes wouldn't find her again.

Once she felt sufficiently far, she sat and rested for a little while, her stomach burning, not from indigestion of the offal she had consumed, but from hunger. She looked down and considered. She unwrapped her leg, disconnecting her stump from AJ's limb. She lifted AJ's leg and smelled it. Something about the vileness of it moved her deeply. She pulled away in disgust but knew that was just a reflex. She raised the calf muscle to her mouth. She spread her teeth and pushed the muscular flesh inside. She bit down hard, tearing a piece of AJ's calf from the bone. She chewed slowly and swallowed. Nancy lowered the leg from her face. Her lips dripped with blood. She smiled, satisfied.

The offing was barred by a black bank of clouds, and the tranquil pathway leading to the uttermost ends of the earth turned somber under an overcast sky— seemed to lead into the heart of an immense darkness.

ABOUT THE AUTHOR

 Jean Chiles Tempi grew up in a world of contradiction. Her mother, Penelope Chiles, is a renowned mime, while her father, a championship yodeler, could shatter glass with his Alpine ululations.

Jean attended Yale University, where she majored in Comparative Literature. Her academic pursuits were heavily influenced by Gothic fiction and real supernatural, much to the chagrin of her conventional professors. She now resides in a creaky old house in Salem, Massachusetts, where she casts spells in pantomime.

When not writing, Jean has taken up crafting faux fur by trapping faux minks, a skill that has made her quite popular among eco-conscious fashionistas. Though she has never married, her relationship status is officially listed as "does as she pleases" on all county documentation.

Jean wrote End Zone 2 in one whirlwind weekend, fueled by an endless pot of black coffee and a slightly alarming number of candied ginger snacks.